LIVING IN *Her Abundance* ON PURPOSE

VOLUME II

8 Stories of Fearless and Confident
Women of Resilience

PRESENTED BY
Kesha D. Haynie

Published by: Abundant Life Coaching Academy, LLC

ISBN: 978-1-7377592-3-2 (Paperback)

Book cover and design by www.fiverr.com/around86
Second printing edition 2025

Kesha D Haynie
PO Box 7508
Chico, CA 95927
www.keshahaynie.com

TABLE OF CONTENTS

Chapter 1:

The Girl in the Window

Simone Williams Young

Have you ever felt as if your life were passing you by and you were watching from the outside in—but it's your life? Almost as if the life you're living is not real? Well, that was me.

As a little girl, I grew up in what some people would call the perfect life. I had a mother and a daddy who loved me, and I was their only child. I had everything I wanted—dolls, dresses, all the trappings of a "good" childhood. But somehow, some way, I always felt a void—like something was missing, like a piece of my soul had been cut out and lost somewhere between the cracks of life.

I've asked myself countless times: When did that feeling begin? Perhaps it started the day my parents' marriage fell apart. I was a daddy's girl—oh, a real daddy's girl. He was my world. His voice, his laugh, the way he'd scoop me up and make me feel like the most important person in the universe. My mother would tell me stories about how, when I was in school, teachers would call and say, "Congratulations, your daughter's getting a brother or sister," but the only sibling I had was the ache of loneliness.

Even in kindergarten and first grade, I got in trouble more times than I could count. My mother sent me to a predominantly Asian and Caucasian private school—a school where everyone else seemed to have money, and no one looked like me. There I was, with my nappy pigtails, acne, and glasses at five years old. I stuck out like a sore thumb. It was traumatizing—I remember it like yesterday. I never felt like I fit in. I never felt like I belonged. It's sad to say, but even at that tender age, I hated life.

Time passed, and I moved from childhood into adolescence and then into my teenage years. But that feeling of being on the outside looking in only intensified. Like I was a visitor in my own story—watching the main character move about but unable to take the stage myself. I was the girl in the window—trapped behind the glass of everyone else's standard.

It didn't help that I could never identify with anything my peers talked about. My mother, wanting to raise me right, only let me listen to Christian music. When other kids talked about the latest movies or the songs everyone was dancing to at school, I sat in silence, a ghost at the table. Eventually, I got smart—I started going over to my dad's house more often. I was still sheltered over there, but at least I could catch a movie or watch a music video to try and keep up. One day, recently, I was scrolling through social media, and a meme appeared of a mad little girl because it was Halloween, but she could only attend Hallelujah Night at church instead of trick-or-treating with friends. Well, that was me! I laugh about it now, but it wasn't funny one bit back then.

Then, one day—almost overnight—I went from an awkward-looking kid to being overdeveloped. It was scary, but I found a strange comfort in it. I used that to try to fill the void I'd felt my whole life. I found it in men, seeking validation from others, trying to quiet the gnawing ache inside that whispered, you'll never be enough. My parents always told me I was special, but I didn't feel it. I felt numb—like I was just existing, watching from that window, waiting for life to begin.

When I was nineteen, I was in fashion college, chasing dreams of becoming a designer or a merchandiser, hoping to break through the glass ceiling I'd built around myself. I thought that was my path to finally proving I was special, that I mattered, that I wasn't just the girl in the window, always looking in on other people's lives. But in the middle of that, I met a man, ten years older than me, who had me completely wrapped around his finger. I was so infatuated with him, convinced he was everything I wanted. His charm, his smile, the way he'd look at me like I was the only woman in the world—it all pulled me in deeper than I'd ever been before. But every time I dealt with him, I ended up feeling dirty, like I was disposable. Like my worth was tied to how much he wanted me in that moment. Still, I kept going back, desperate for the attention I'd been missing, as if he held the answer to the emptiness I carried inside. He didn't. He only deepened the void that had always lived inside me.

Then I got pregnant. My dreams shattered like fragile glass, and I dropped out of college. Between caring for a baby and carrying the weight of discouragement, I felt like the odds were stacked against me. Every morning, I'd look in the mirror at the girl in the window staring back at me with sad, questioning eyes. *What was I thinking?* The voice in my head wouldn't let up. *There's nothing special about you. Look at you. You couldn't even protect your own dreams.* But before I could even begin to pick up the pieces, I found myself pregnant again. This time, the shame and guilt wrapped around my heart like chains, and the darkness crept in, whispering that maybe my children would be better off without me.

I was my parents' only child and the oldest of all the nieces and cousins on both sides. People expected great things from me. I was supposed to be the one who made it, the one who showed everyone how it was done. But the search for something to fill that void left me looking like a failure—a young, unwed mother of two with nothing in my life to show for it but my children. My friends, my parents, and my grandparents were worried about me. I wasn't the same anymore. The girl they knew, the one they thought was so full of promise, was gone, replaced by someone they didn't recognize.

But even through all that, I loved my children more than anything in this world. They were my lifeline, the one thing that kept me from giving up altogether. Even when I felt like I'd failed them, I tried to give them everything I had. I'd hold them close, praying that somehow my love could make up for every mistake I'd made. Sometimes, I'd overcompensate—buying them things, trying to create memories, anything to make the guilt hurt less. Because deep down, I carried the guilt of why they were even here in the first place. I blamed myself for their struggles, convinced that my bad decisions had sentenced them to a life they didn't deserve. I felt like I had ruined everything—like my life, my children's lives, my family's legacy. I carried the weight of generations on my shoulders. The girl in the window—that silent, unseen version of me—just watched, wondering if I'd ever find my way out, wondering if I'd ever believe that there was still hope for me.

But even in the darkest places, one thing never left me: I loved God with all my heart. Deep down, I have always known I possess a special gift. Some people called me a psychic, but I knew better—I was sensitive to the Spirit, able to sense things others couldn't. I noticed that people loved to talk to me—even grown women would pour out their hearts to me about their marriages and struggles. As a teenager, children who wanted to run away from home would talk to me. I befriended the outcasts, the ones no one else wanted, the troubled souls. I looked out for them, even when I couldn't look out for myself.

There was a time in my life, around eighteen, when I gave my virginity away. Everyone kept telling me how special it was, how it was reserved for my husband, how it was a part of my value as a woman. But how could I value something like that when I didn't even feel like my life had any value at all? So I gave it away. I just wanted it to be gone so it wouldn't be hanging over my head anymore. I hated myself, and I hated it. I didn't want to hear one more time why I should keep it—another lie, another trick of the enemy, another burden that made me feel like I'd never measure up.

The girl in the window. I kept remembering that feeling of always living my life the way others wanted me to—feeling like everyone expected me to be perfect because of all the opportunities that were afforded to me. Most people reminded me of that, and to be honest, I just wanted to punch them. Why could everyone else see that I was special, but I couldn't see it for myself?

There was also a time when a prophet came to me and said, "Your life is worth more than just having babies. God has use of you, and He wants to use you." I think that was after I got married the first time. And let me tell you, I felt exactly that—like I was only good for sex and babies, like I was just a trophy on a shelf, a conquest for a man who didn't know how to love me. It felt like nothing good could come from me except through my children. So why would God want to use someone like me?

And the same prophet who had given me that word at my wedding shower had also come to me, possibly years before I got married, and said, "God wants to use you." At times, I'd literally run from her because it felt like she could see right through me, every secret, every shameful thing. She always had a word from the Lord, and all I wanted was to be left alone to self-destruct in peace.

Yet even in that mess, I had a fear of God. I still loved Him. But I felt so unworthy, so dirty, and so lost. The things I had done, the things I had seen and experienced, and the poor decisions I had made all weighed on me. I felt like my kids had suffered because of my choices. I suffered because of them, too. It was like a constantly revolving door of self-pity and condemnation. I couldn't even forgive myself. I think I finally forgave myself in my 40s for all the bad decisions I made, even the ones that were good decisions but still had consequences. I'd second-guess everything, and the self-condemnation would creep back in.

Later, I married a man I knew wasn't God's best for me. But I settled because I didn't believe I was worth any better. And I did love him in my own way. However, by the time I realized he wasn't the one for me, I was pregnant. I thought I had to make it work. But the truth was, I was miserable, depressed, and even suicidal. I made poor choices to appear happy. I put on a smile while my soul was crumbling.

Even at my bridal shower, there was a prophet there who said—boldly, in front of everyone—that the husband I was about to marry was not God's best for me. She said God would give me the desires of my heart because I wanted him so badly, but she warned me: "If you marry him, you're going to stay on your face in His face," meaning I'd be spending my days on my knees, praying for strength to endure. And man, oh man, did that word come to pass.

I had to deal with alcoholism, narcissistic behaviors, a loss of income, cars repossessed due to his drinking, and much more. My health suffered under the weight of it all, and I felt trapped. I married him because of my faith in God, because even though I didn't do everything right, I feared the Lord. I already had a child with him and didn't want that child to suffer the way my other children had because their fathers weren't in their lives. I wanted this one to have his father. I knew this man loved me—there was no question about that. But he had his own demons to face, and once we married, those demons became our demons.

I inherited spiritual warfare that wasn't mine to fight. Because I became one with someone I wasn't supposed to, I found myself battling forces I didn't invite into my life. And so I suffered—until God made a way of escape.

I remember we were about to be evicted, and I cried out to God for help. I was working two jobs while my husband wasn't working at all, yet I couldn't keep us afloat. One day, God told me clearly: "Get up, take a $50 money order to the property management company, and hurry—put it in the drop box before they open." I did just that. Later that day, I got the call: we were being evicted. However, because they cashed the money order, they couldn't just put us out right then and there. Instead, they had to serve us another three-day notice, which gave us time to gather our belongings and prepare to leave.

The significance of that moment was that I'd been too afraid to leave him—I'd tried everything to make him leave me first, but he'd always get aggressive if he felt any rejection from me. Just a few nights before that, I'd sat on the bed and cried out to God: "I can't do this anymore. I want to leave, but I know you hate divorce. Please, deliver me." That's when God gave me the instructions to make a way of escape.

We ended up living in two separate places. We had seven children between us, blending our families, but he stayed at his mom's house while I stayed at my dad's. I started looking for a place for us to move to, but he was difficult, resistant, and manipulative—and at that moment, it felt like God knocked on my head and said: "If you move him into your new place, you'll never get him out." And right then, I knew what God had done for me. I decided to move on my own, and God made a way for me to escape.

But the journey to that revelation was neither quick nor easy. A turning point arrived much later in my life, years after high school, after the heartbreaks, and after dreams that felt like they'd been snatched away. For the first time in a long while, I felt utterly defeated; my dad passed away in December 2016, and then in February 2017, I underwent a hysterectomy. I believe all the stress I endured caused my fibroids to become active. I was like the woman with the issue of blood, going to the hospital where my blood count should have been at 12, but when I went, it was at 5 or 4, resulting in constant blood transfusions and pain. After my dad passed, I was supposed to receive an inheritance from him, but it seemed my family found a way to intercept it and keep it for themselves. At that time, my dad was financially supporting my children and also planning to help my son through college. Not only did they take the money, but they didn't think about me at all. There was no outreach to see how I was doing after my father passed; it just felt like I was completely forgotten—weddings, no invitation; baby showers, no invitation, just nothing.

In November 2017, I moved to Texas in hopes of making a change. I could get my mind right and do something for my youngest children. However, things took a turn when I suffered an injury. I shattered my ankle and had to return home. Another failure, I thought. The jobs weren't an issue; I couldn't work or pay rent, so I had to go back to California. Once I was home, the depression intensified, and I truly wanted to die. I felt so tired and worn out. I prayed to fall asleep and never wake up. The girl in the window—she was back, stronger than ever, whispering lies that I wasn't enough, that I'd never be enough, and that I was just a complete failure to myself and my children.

But even in that place, my spirit was stirring. Something inside me kept nagging at me, pushing me to get to the church my mother had been attending in California. I felt it so strongly in my spirit that I couldn't ignore it. I got to California on a Friday, and by Monday, I knew I had to be in that church. That nagging feeling was God's way of saving me because death was standing at my doorstep, ready to claim me.

How many people know that death and life are in the power of the tongue? God will give you the desires of your heart, but in that moment, my heart desired to die. And I know now that stirring was God's last way of saving me before the end, I thought I wanted.

Entering that church—Wrecking Crew for Christ Holiness Church in Los Angeles, California—broken, with a shattered ankle and a shattered soul, marked a turning point I didn't even realize I needed. Senior Pastor Chief Apostle Michael L. Rowles looked at me—no judgment, no condemnation—and said, "I pray for your strength." Then he told me, "If you hadn't come here today, you would have been gone in a few days' time." What he didn't know was that I had been praying for the death angel to find me. I could feel its presence, and I wasn't afraid to die, only scared of what would become of my children. They were the only reason I stayed alive. But even they almost couldn't keep me here. I was at peace with leaving at that time. I was tired. But God said, Not so. My saving grace was God leading me to that church, where I was eventually ordained as a prophet and now help others—all glory be to God.

I didn't know then how the pull and tug to go to Wrecking Crew was tied to my destiny. It wasn't just about showing up at church; it was about being planted in a place where I could learn and apply everything I knew, as well as all that I didn't even realize I needed. I wasn't fixed right away, but I was given tools—tools to work on myself, to build a strong foundation in my faith. Jesus said in Matthew 7:24-25 (KJV), "Therefore whosoever heareth these sayings of mine, and doeth them, I will liken him unto a wise man, which built his house upon a rock: and the rain descended, and the floods came, and the winds blew, and beat upon that house; and it fell not: for it was founded upon a rock." That's what Wrecking Crew did for me—it provided me with that rock-solid foundation so that when the storms came, I didn't just crumble. I had endurance.

Little did I know I would need that endurance more than ever. On August 1, 2020, my son was killed by gun violence. That's a pain no mother should ever have to bear. Yet, I was surprised by how strong I was. Before I came to the church, something like this would have destroyed me. I would have fallen apart completely. However, I was surprised by how well I held up, not just for myself, but for those watching my journey unfold publicly. People approached me, saying how strong they thought I was and how they couldn't imagine surviving what I had endured. The truth is, I am not strong, but the One who lives in me is even stronger. For 1 John 4:4 (KJV) declares, "Ye are of God, little children, and have overcome them: because greater is he that is in you, than he that is in the world."

It wasn't my natural strength that carried me; it was His supernatural strength in me that made it possible to stand. Philippians 4:13 (KJV) says, "I can do all things through Christ which strengtheneth me." Without Him, I could have done nothing.

I also didn't know that the man I had needed all my life, my husband, was in that very church. He nurtures me, teaches me, loves me, and is patient with me. He loved me into healing. It was as if he were a gift from God Himself, a reward for all the pain and suffering I had endured. Proverbs 10:22 (KJV) says, "The blessing of the Lord, it maketh rich, and he addeth no sorrow with it."

One requirement from him was that I open up and let him see all the broken places I had kept hidden from everyone else. He wanted to love me fully—not just the put-together parts but the raw, real, broken parts, too. Now, I no longer identify with the girl in the window. I am no longer on the outside looking in. Now, I am living my life through the eyes of God. I see myself the way He sees me. I'm learning how to do that more and more each day. Just like my pastor would say, "I'm not like I should be, but I'm nowhere like I used to be," and I thank God for that.

And yet—here I stand today, walking in the office of the prophet. I now understand that feeling unworthy was a weapon of the enemy used to prevent me from recognizing that I am valuable to God, a threat to his kingdom. The enemy knew that if I ever acknowledged the power within me, I'd be unstoppable.

I am also the founder and publisher of Young at Heart Publishing LLC. If I had given up, those who are assigned to me through my endeavors would have been lost. I think about that often: what would have happened to the countless authors, the grieving souls, the prophetic voices God entrusted me to help birth? Their destiny is tied to my obedience. That's the kind of responsibility that will make you put on your armor and fight every demon that dares to tell you that you don't matter.

If you're reading this and feel like you're still that girl—or that boy—in the window, I want to speak life to you right now. God says, "You are not forgotten." You may feel like you're on the outside looking in, but He's calling you to step out of the window and into His promises. That feeling of being stuck, overlooked, or unworthy? It's a lie from the enemy to keep you from walking in your destiny.

Psalm 139:14 reminds us: "I praise you because I am fearfully and wonderfully made, your works are wonderful, I know that full well." You are His masterpiece, crafted with intention, called with purpose.

The enemy would love nothing more than to keep you paralyzed in self-doubt and shame. But God is lifting you up. He's breaking every chain that's tried to hold you back. He's opening every window you thought was sealed shut and saying, "Come out, daughter. Come out, son. I have work for you to do."

Isaiah 61:3 says, "To all who mourn in Zion, He will give a crown of beauty for ashes, the oil of joy for mourning, and a garment of praise instead of a spirit of despair." That's your promise today. Beauty for your ashes. Joy for your sorrow. Purpose for your pain.

So, my sister, my brother—if you've been the one sitting in the window, it's time to rise. It's time to step through that glass, even if it's scary, even if you're trembling. Because on the other side of your fear is your freedom. On the other side of your doubt is your destiny.

I pray that this chapter serves as a prophetic mirror, showing you not just who you were but who God says you are. A warrior. A healer. A voice. A threat to the enemy's camp. And most of all—a child of the Most High God.

No more windows. No more waiting. No more wondering if you're worthy.

You are.

You always have been.

You always will be.

So, step into the light because the world is waiting for you.

Chapter 2:

BUT GOD

Krista Geddes

First chapter: Stream of Changes

I was born on August 15, 1979, just nine months after my parents' wedding. That day, my mother said there was a lightning storm with no rain. She believed it was heaven celebrating my birth.

At the age of 10, I was baptized at Calvary Chapel in San Francisco, California, on Easter morning at sunrise, in the Pacific Ocean—a place and moment I had no idea were historically significant until years later.

As a little girl, I was joyful, deeply obedient, and loved Jesus with everything in me. I led other kids to Christ at recess and church camp. My father held a PhD and was almost genius-level smart, but emotionally, he had the capacity of a teaspoon. I grew up in an upper-middle-class Christian bubble carefully curated by my mother. We had no access to secular TV or music. Our television was locked up. We were allowed Saturday morning cartoons, the Disney Sunday movie, and the occasional episode of Star Trek: The Next Generation. Music was limited to Christian artists, 80s and 90s country, and oldies—but even "Sixty Minute Man" was banned.

My mom and dad taught me to perform every task with excellence. My childhood was filled with swimming, gymnastics, and competition. I was naturally athletic and was recruited by the U.S. Gymnastics League at a young age. However, my mother wouldn't let me leave for Texas to train. I shifted to swimming, competing throughout high school. I began working at a young age, cleaning houses by 9 or 10 to save for college. I rode my bike uphill to clean, was inspected with white gloves, and took pride in doing it well.

My upbringing reflected an extreme Christian parenting model from a popular movement that influenced every aspect of our home life. It wasn't until I turned 18 that I saw my mother deviate from that path when she read Harry Potter and, to her surprise, concluded that it upheld Christian values, despite what the mainstream "Christian" church teachers she followed insisted.

School was tough socially. I didn't fit in with the cool kids and was bullied relentlessly. On my last day of elementary school, instead of saying goodbye, my entire class barked at me, mocking me one last time. Yet, in that pain, I discovered my first callings: justice and advocacy. I felt outraged when I saw a teacher mistreating a classmate who smelled bad and wore the same clothes every day. The teacher ridiculed him publicly and even slammed another kid into a bookshelf. I defended the boy and was sent to detention—my first discipline ever. My parents supported me. I knew then I wanted to fight for people like Jesus did.

As a child, I was captivated by stories of American slavery and the Civil Rights Movement. Harriet Tubman became my hero, not just for what she did but for how she did it: by hearing the voice of God and obeying it without hesitation. Just as Harriet inspired my sense of fearless obedience, Mother Teresa stirred in me the desire to live like Jesus—close to the suffering, never above them, and filled with joy in serving. Her life showed me what it meant to be the hands and feet of Christ. Her quote, "I am just a pencil in the hand of God," became one of my lifelong mottos. I set up Bible studies in schools and consumed scripture passionately before I was even a teenager.

We moved to Alameda in the 5th grade. I didn't fit in, but I found my people—a misfit group I still remember fondly. I was book-smart, very sheltered, and honest to a fault. However, that would all begin to change in high school.

High school marked a turning point in my life. My parents divorced, and everything I understood about identity, safety, and purpose unraveled. I didn't just question who I was; I started to believe I was nothing. I transformed from an obedient, Jesus-loving girl into a full-blown rebel.

And yet, even in that rebellion, I still performed. I was a varsity player in every sport I tried—swimming, diving, boys' varsity water polo, dance team, flag team, and soccer, among others. As a freshman, I even took a senior's spot on the varsity swim team. I won numerous medals and trophies. This was particularly impressive, as my school competed against elite, wealthy schools across the Bay Area, consistently winning against the best of the best. As for academics, I enrolled in all the college prep courses available and worked hard to maintain excellent grades. Despite being dyslexic, I often tutored friends in subjects that challenged them. I had to work harder to learn, but that made me even more determined. I built a near-perfect college résumé, truly an overachiever on paper. I also worked throughout high school—scooping ice cream at a local shop and working at a horse ranch, where I gave trail rides and taught horseback riding at kids' camps. I balanced academics, jobs, sports, and band competitions with an overwhelming drive to excel in everything I did to secure college scholarships. However, when the time came to apply to colleges, I did not dedicate enough effort to my essays and applications. My father, the night before applications were due, helped write a little something. Still, I mostly missed every deadline, despite all the preparation and hard work I had put in since the age of 9. As a result, I followed my mother to Chico after graduation and enrolled in a junior college. That one choice shifted everything.

1. Up until then, I had been a "crazy rebellious teen who still got everything done." However, after moving to Chico, that unraveling process accelerated. I didn't just experiment with rebellion—I dove into it completely. I became a full-blown hood rat. Partying, drinking, boys, broken friendships, and inner chaos became my new normal. I started hanging out with gang members and drug dealers. It wasn't just rebellion, it was self-destruction. I experienced the darkest sides of that world.

2. I had a man rip the cords out of my stereo and hogtie me with them on my bed, making sure the door was open so everyone could see me.

3. One man asked me to play Russian Roulette. When I refused, he removed all but one bullet from the gun and chased me around the house, pulling the trigger repeatedly. By some miracle, none of the chambers contained the bullet. I don't remember how it ended.
4. I was forced to lie in bed for hours while a man held a Tec-9 semi-automatic gun to my head, just because he could.

On the day my four-year-old special needs brother died and my mother was undergoing a fifth surgery from prior medical complications, a dangerous man called me saying he was coming to kill me. I begged him not to. He said if the door were locked, it would be worse. I replied, "Can you kill me tomorrow? My brother just died." He said no. I hid my little sister and waited. He never showed up.

I concealed my shame behind a mask of false confidence, gritty toughness, and survival instinct. Eventually, I became pregnant with my first child, Zoe. Her father was volatile and dangerous. We weren't in a relationship; he visited a few times a week to smoke and engage in sex. I didn't even have his phone number. One day, he locked me in my room for an hour, claiming it was because he loved me. I laughed at him. When I was nine months pregnant and mentioned I was considering adoption, he lifted me up by my head.

I seriously considered giving Zoe up for adoption because I was still deeply entrenched in the hood life, and I knew she deserved better. I had seen too many parents bring children into the world, hoping the baby would change them, but it rarely did. I didn't want to gamble with her future. She deserved more than a broken mother trying to figure things out. I believed her well-being shouldn't depend on whether I managed to get it together or not.

Zoe was born on November 28, 2000. After two months of early labor, 30 hours of active labor, several hours of pushing, and finally, an emergency C-section, she was here. The moment I saw her face, my heart said, "Whatever it takes to change." She was my baby. And I changed quickly. Her life marked the beginning of my rebirth.

Motherhood brought a kind of broken healing. I loved Zoe fiercely and wanted to give her a life unlike my own. But her earliest years were marked by trauma I couldn't have foreseen. I began to notice signs that something was wrong, she would flinch, withdraw, and cry in ways that didn't match her age. I realized that someone in my mother's home was abusing her. I ran. I had ten days to find a new place to live. That's when I realized I was pregnant again. I didn't even know it until the chaos hit. Now, I wasn't just protecting Zoe; I was also protecting the new life growing inside me. With no money and nowhere safe to go, a family offered me a rented room. They didn't just provide us a roof when we had nowhere else to turn; they gave my kids a big family for years. Because of this family, my children were able to enjoy a big, everyday family life. We celebrated every holiday, birthday, and BBQ with them. They always included my children as if they were theirs. It was God's provision and coverage despite my poor choices.

I was still young, trying to figure out how to parent while healing from my trauma. I often had flashbacks and would fall apart emotionally as old wounds surfaced. I tried to hold those breakdowns in until my kids were asleep. I'd go into the bathroom, shut the door, and quietly flip out, processing years of pain behind a closed door. But Zoe always seemed to know. Somehow, no matter how quiet I was, she would wake up and find me. She'd sit with me in silence or offer comfort far beyond her years. She was forced to grow up too fast and could sense when I was breaking, even when I tried to hide it. But we made it. We laughed. We sang. I worked jobs, went to school, and gave Zoe and Rhema the type of love I never had. I drew inspiration from my parents' excellent examples of how to love and teach kids while avoiding the mistakes they made. I eventually started working at law firms as a lowly file clerk when I was pregnant with Rhema around early 2002. I continued working at law firms, attending school, and raising my daughters with no family support. I always made sure their homework was done well; they had extracurricular activities, and I taught them as much as I could at home. I tried my best to make life fun despite having no money. Some of our favorite inexpensive activities were spending time by the pool at our apartment. Hardly anyone used it, and for over five years, it was our little retreat, complete with a good pool, food, and fun movies at home afterward. I always made sure Friday night was family night, and Saturday morning included cartoons. We would also visit the Bear Hole, a local swimming hole. It was fun with people and music, and it felt like we were in a different world on vacation. Then it was cheap Mexican food, grabbing a Red Box movie, and heading home. Perfect staycation! Sometimes, for a fun day, we would get 7-11 Slurpees and snacks and drive around with loud music, looking at the most expensive houses for fun; it just cost the snacks and extra gas. We also had two restaurants that were affordable if we did it right, so my kids could enjoy the "eat in a restaurant" experience. One place still knows us, despite my kids being adults now, because they saw me go through law school and study at their restaurant. My kids thrived in school and extracurricular activities.

From a young age, I knew I was called to fight for civil rights, and I wanted my sweet mixed, brown babies to have that, too. That fire never went out. In those early years in Chico, before Trayvon Martin and the second Civil Rights movement, I took my daughters to Martin Luther King Jr. Day marches many years ago. We joined the small crowd that walked from downtown Chico to a little church. I remember sitting in that sanctuary and crying out to God again, this time asking, "Why did You have me born in this era? I feel like you trained me for a civil rights battle that doesn't exist."

But God knew.

I was born in the perfect era. Right on time. Right at the beginning of the second Civil Rights Movement. Right when the world needed both a Harriet Tubman and an Anne Frank—

someone to lead and someone to witness—with the fearlessness and determination represented by these two women.

Second chapter: Changes

I ended up working for a wonderful man who changed our lives. I learned a great deal about being a paralegal from working in offices rather than in school. I was already doing paralegal work when my boss asked if I wanted to get my paralegal certificate to learn the "why" behind the "what" I was doing. I worked for him for years and learned a great deal. During my time at Chico State, I earned my paralegal certificate. I won the Best Brief award in Chico State's Moot Court competition. I almost won the arguments, but my partner did not do well. Finally, one day, the conversation that changed everything started with my boss saying, "The question isn't if you're going to law school, but when?" There were no scholarships or student loans available to me, but my boss stepped in to make it possible. My boss was offering to pay for my law school tuition.

On the first day of class, I couldn't even walk into the building. I didn't believe I belonged with the 'smart people.' I sat outside, crying on the ground behind the building, convinced I didn't belong there. Eventually, I found the strength and courage to go inside, and thus began my life-changing journey. I never would have had the opportunity to attend law school if it weren't for my boss and his wife. They watched my kids, covered expenses, and stepped in where every traditional path failed. My kids were surrounded by a fantastic group of people who loved them and introduced them to a whole new world. My boss and his wife were brilliant, free-spirited individuals. They lived in Forest Ranch and would take my kids mushroom hunting, sledding, and teach them how to cook, among many other things. Because of their support, my kids became even more well-rounded and well-loved than I could have provided without family support. But God!

During law school, I received a call that my mother had breast cancer. I was informed she had just undergone surgery and was in the hospital, and things were severe enough that I should visit her. I hadn't seen my mother in years, and once again, I was reminded why. I walked into her room and told her about all my accomplishments in law school, including being at the top of my class. The exponential growth of the law firm I worked for was primarily due to my hard work and innovative efforts as a paralegal. My mother's response was to start crying. I was confused and asked her why she was crying. She said, "All I can think about is the poor babies that you are abandoning." Her only comment was that I was abandoning my children by working full-time and attending law school. I left the hospital feeling confused, defeated, and brokenhearted.

I ended up graduating as valedictorian—so far ahead of my classmates that they were competing for second place. But law school, just like everything in my life, came with severe trials and pain to push through. My final year of law school was brutal. I was so sick that I often had to Skype into class from the ER. During horrible weeks of the month, I needed IV pain meds to function. Law school and the State Bar have strict rules regarding class attendance, and I was hospitalized so frequently that it seemed I might miss too many days to graduate. But I was determined. I bought a second laptop and asked a classmate to bring it to class while I connected from the hospital or ER—so technically, I was present. As a result of that workaround, the school later established a formal policy permitting remote attendance. When I wasn't in the hospital, a classmate would drive me to school and help me carry my pillows. I would lie nearly flat in the back of the class, laptop on my lap, doing whatever it took to finish. I was so far ahead that I could have barely passed my fourth year and still been valedictorian. Due to medical complications, however, I was unable to study or sit for the bar exam with my class. I had to wait until the next bar cycle when I was finally healed enough to take it. I passed my first try!!

My healing before taking the bar exam, after being sick throughout my last year of law school, was yet another miracle, just like the miracles of God in the Old Testament. I remember being home and in a lot of pain while my kids were with the nanny at youth group. I got a call from the nanny freaking out. Kids were getting hit with the holy ghost. Kids, even the super cool football guys, were lying on the ground just praising God out of it. She called me because she had never seen anything like it. I decided I had to go to the church with a strong urge instead of having her take the kids home. When I got there, I felt like I was supposed to ask one of the women to pray for me. I knelt before the altar, and she kneeled behind me and started praying. I felt something come up out of my stomach and out of my mouth, and the pain that had been plaguing me during my last year of law school for about 7 months was gone!!!

After law school, due to illness, I became an attorney without a job. Despite being a valedictorian with over 20 years of experience, working from a file clerk to a high-level paralegal, I was able to secure a position at a firm that went from making about $100,000 a year to $400,000 a year when I became ill. I also handled almost everything, from phone calls and billing to filing and complex paralegal work, all independently. However, I was unable to secure a job. I was back to standing in food lines and hustling (legal, of course). I created three résumés: one with all my accolades, degree, and experience, one with a lower-level degree, and one with nothing to try to get a job delivering pizzas or something similar. Nothing was working. However, I've been working since the age of 10, if you recall, with two house cleaning jobs, so I was determined and ready to do any work to support my family, with no ego. I should tell you that during a significant portion of this time, I also had two different "stray" high school students living with me and supporting them.

At this time, we attended a wonderful (though flawed) Black Baptist Church in town. We were there every Sunday; my daughters were in the children's choir, and later, I joined the choir. I remember bringing my law school flashcards to church to try to do both. So, everyone at church had seen me push for 4 years to get my Doctorate and become an attorney. To earn some money, I asked around at church to see if anyone had any odd jobs. A deacon at my church offered me odd jobs, such as pruning his roses, and always paid me extra for them. I got a job on Craigslist to help someone move. I also cleaned my pastor's house, etc., etc. One month, the additional jobs were not enough to make rent. I was about 75 dollars short, but I had mailed out the check. I realized I had to go and panhandle. With my now-legal brain, I knew to research how to panhandle legally. I then got a big sign that said, "Single Mom, College Grad, Short on rent." I will never forget the first dollar I took. I started crying. This woman and her husband parked, came, and walked up to me to talk. She talked about her kids, encouraged me, and hugged me. She gave me $20.00 when she first gave me a dollar. Another man also parked and approached me. He told me the same thing happened to his fiancée, and now he supports her. So many people loved me, But God! I made 85.00 that day, more than enough! O and I got a nice tan, lol. As good as God was, don't miss where the real blessing is in this situation. This is the real lesson. I learned what it felt like to have to panhandle, to stand out on the street for everyone to see and judge, hundreds of cars, seeing you at your worst; I felt naked, humiliated, a failure, etc. However, I saw God provide me with overwhelming love and support, not just financially but also from others. So the gold???? I can help others, relate to them, and share a real story of how God loved me and was faithful to get me through. This changed my very soul and gave me a mighty sword to love people and give them an example of God's faithfulness.

Around this time, I got a more regular job taking care of and cleaning for a wonderful old lady who gave her husband some time off. I fell in love with her. She would call her friends and tell them she had an attorney cleaning her house, bahaha. I was working as an attorney, picking up my first few cases. I would get paid $10.00 an hour and $100.00 an hour on the same day. I remember one day, I was deep into a pedicure for "my old lady" when my phone rang. I was practicing law, and it was also my work phone, so I answered, "Law Office." It was the DA wanting to discuss a criminal case I had and see if we could settle it. I scooted away from the pedicure, grateful that the attorney on the other line couldn't see me, as I was wearing a tank top and oversized basketball shorts, which were wet from the pedicure. I ended up settling the case and went back to my old lady and her toes!

Soon after I obtained my license to practice law, my oldest daughter fell ill. We ended up at UC Davis for a total of 3 months. We were sent home a few times, but we lived there for the most part. I had a few clients and did my best to work at the hospital, handling legal matters and taking calls in the hallway. I had an 11-year-old who had horrific belly pain. She was in so much pain that they tried to put her to sleep with meds at night. They had such massive amounts of different meds to get her to sleep that they had special meds on the floor just for her to restart her heart if it went out from the meds. The crazy part is that they still could not put her to sleep. She would scream for hours, clawing the mattress and writhing in pain every night. It was torture to watch. Around the middle of all this, we were sent home for a week. During this time, my youngest ended up needing her appendix taken out. No breaks.

A sacrifice that had to be made, given a child who may never recover, was to give up being an attorney, even after four years of hard work in school and five months of studying for the bar. I had to give it all up. I was now going to have to figure out how to be my daughter's full-time care provider. I had to drop the Salt and know my worth, aka Salt, came from God, not a degree or career. God calls us the "salt of the earth," which means we are valued and have a sense of identity. Salt was also used as currency. I needed to chase the Salt that came from God, regardless of a law firm. My Salt came from God alone.

After three months, we returned to our upstairs apartment. I had a child who needed to be carried up and down the stairs and required assistance walking to the bathroom. I remember the day at church; we had been staying home because Zoe couldn't walk or be left alone. Suddenly, I got a powerful, undeniable feeling that I was supposed to take Zoe to church and surrender my rights to her health or even relief from pain to God. I envisioned Abraham placing his firstborn son, whom he had waited over one hundred years for, on the altar. The feeling was so intense that I was nearly frantic to find a way to church. I managed to get a neighbor to help drive us there. I carried my 11-year-old like a baby and laid her down in the truck. Then, I carried her to a pew in the church, where she lay down. When it was time for people to go to the altar to give testimony, etc., I took my firstborn baby to the altar and laid her down since she couldn't sit or stand. I told the church that over 20 doctors had informed us that Zoe might be in nonstop pain for the rest of her life and had sent us home to learn how to cope with it. I told the church that God loves my daughter more than I do and that whatever plans He has for her life are good. I laid down my desires in place of His. That very week, she suddenly started walking and feeling better after months of suffering. God is still in the miracle business.

God used every bit of my story to birth a career in justice and ministry, where I'd advocate for the broken with the same fire that had carried me through the darkest places of my own life. BUT GOD, I ended up passing the bar on my first attempt, even with my severe dyslexia. I did, of course, in Krista-like fashion; I spelled my own name wrong, though. Looking back, Satan stole my ability to go to college and follow that four-year dream I had been working on since I was nine years old. God gave it back to me, "pushed down and shaken together." (Luke 6:38). If I had followed the standard timeline four years right after school, then law school, I would have been 25 when I graduated from law school, which was never my plan to attend if I was perfect with no breaks. I ended up being 33, but I had 6 years of experience as a high-level paralegal and 9 years of experience in law firms. I was FARTHER AHEAD!! "God, your God, will restore everything you lost; he'll have compassion on you; he'll come back and pick up the pieces from all the places where you were scattered." (Deuteronomy 30:3). Because of this, I was able to start my own law firm right out of college.

My firm grew fast from word of mouth alone. I had a motto that I put on my business cards, which said, "Human first, attorney second." When I eventually got my current, big, beautiful office, I framed my last two paper food stamps and put them on the wall under my degree. My firm grew so fast that, by word of mouth alone, I had my cards and a pen that said, "I stole this pen from my attorney Krista Geddes," and included my contact information. I had several significant cases. One made front-page news locally twice, and the other was suing the United States as a second-year attorney and beating them at the most complex and most complicated civil motions. I prayed not that my firm would grow or I would get cases, but that Jesus would give me my "assignments," not just random business. I told my clients I did not care if their check was good; I would only stay if I felt the argument was honorable. Many clients showed up and had the same story: "I prayed, and someone handed me your card."

Around 2016, several life-altering events collided at once. My brother, Jordan, and my foster son had already been part of our lives for a while, and their presence added to the rhythm and heartbeat of our home. We had laughter, healing, and a sense of a new beginning. Soon after this, I got into my first serious relationship—something I had tried so hard to avoid until my kids graduated from high school. I had always promised myself I wouldn't bring anyone serious into their lives until they were older. But it didn't happen that way. Terror hit soon after.

That season nearly broke me. Zoe's breakdown came suddenly, just before Easter, when she was around 16 or 17. The day before the breakdown, she had run five miles and lifted weights for two hours. The very next day, she couldn't walk, eat, or drink. That moment began nearly two years of horror: graphic, realistic, and exhausting nightmares every night, with hospital visits to keep her eating and hydrated. Watching your child live through trauma is agony—watching them relive it every night is a torment only God could carry me through.

I was also in my first serious relationship during this time. We had moved in together not long after Zoe's collapse, and Jordan and my foster son came into our home. I was running a law firm with two full-time staff members, taking on heartbreaking family law cases, and caring for several teens who came in and out of our lives needing healing. My ex, whom I later learned was manipulating behind the scenes, kept showing flashes of the "dark side" he always bragged about having. The more broken he acted, the harder I tried to love him into healing. But I was losing myself. He worked against me at home while I tried to hold everything together, all the while laughing behind my back and destroying what was most valuable to me, my relationship with my kids, especially my youngest. I was a flawed mother to my youngest, Rhema, during this critical time in her life. She did not make it easy and has always struggled with oppositional defiance issues. My ex was poisoning her, but still, I was standing alone for letting her down. I had become a screaming monster too many times. I had very little to give her because I was drowning. Thank God we have been repairing our relationship and are closer than ever.

Eventually, my body crashed from the weight of the trauma. My body couldn't take it. I collapsed.

It wasn't until I finally freed myself from that relationship in 2019 that God began to show me where I had gone wrong. In the quiet, I saw my codependency clearly. I had been trying to save and sacrifice my way to worthiness. God showed me memory after memory where my need to fix or please had caused pain to those I loved. I made a vow that day—if anything in me was hurting my kids, it had to die, even if that thing lived deep inside me.

2020 was physically excruciating. I cried in level 10 pain for hours a day. I couldn't walk. Couldn't cook. And yet—God. In the depths of suffering, I heard His voice more clearly than ever. My value hadn't changed. My ministry hadn't stopped. I was no less useful to Him from a bed than I was from a pulpit. So I asked Him every day: "Okay, God, what are we up to?" That year became one of the most powerful seasons of spiritual growth in my life. COVID relief helped sustain me financially. I couldn't get disability, but God made a way.

By early 2021, the doctors FINALLY started figuring out what was wrong with me. After years of being dismissed, I was validated. And thank God—it wasn't an autoimmune disease like they'd feared. It turned out I had ignored and suppressed a million different injuries, all of which needed surgery. I became Humpty Dumpty. In the last five years, I've had over 15 surgeries or major procedures—and I'm still facing more.

Some of them were shocking. My left elbow tendon was barely attached from an injury over a decade ago, with scarring and bone buildup so bad the surgeon said it was the worst he'd ever seen. I was still weightlifting with it. When everything collapsed, I couldn't even wash my hands without bracing my elbow. I dropped pots and pans and had radiating pain and numbness in both hands, made worse by carpal tunnel.

Both of my ankles had floating bone fragments. My tendons were so loose that my feet collapsed inward, and the surgeon could easily pull the joint in and out. He had to saw and scrape each bone connection using his whole body—he even demonstrated as if he were sawing through a tree.

Then there was my neck—my most debilitating injury. I have stenosis and pinched nerves from years of being thrown by horses, hitting the ground in gymnastics and dance, rollerblading tricks, and all kinds of wipeouts. The pain was excruciating. I've had nerves burned in two joints, both sides, several times. One doctor told me to "work out until I smelled bad," repeating it until I was crying. I tried to explain that I use all my energy daily to work, run errands, and take care of basic household tasks. Even showering was sometimes too much.

But God. I'm still in pain, but I'm healing. Compared to 2020, I am a new person. I can work, run an errand, and still sit in the living room. Before, I could maybe make it to the office for two hours, then spend the rest of the day rocking in pain. I can even lift my sister now and be okay. I'm still in pain every second of every day. My "pain mileage" still greatly limits me.

And just as I began putting my body back together, God was about to reunite my family, too, because in 2024, I was reunited with my siblings.

As you know, my parents divorced in the mid-1990s. When I started high school, my mother began adopting children with special needs. That's how my siblings Max and Korin came into our lives. Korin was just a baby when she arrived; I was in high school, and from the beginning, she felt like my own. I fed her, held her, and loved her as if she were mine. She also became Jordan's best friend—inseparable since childhood. Max, though more reserved, was still our brother and deeply loved. My mother adopted my little sister Nattie and another brother, who is the one I lost. All the kids were between 2 and 5 years old when we adopted them. I was around 18 and in Chico, hitting the streets hard. Fast forward to now, and I have custody of three of my siblings.

Eight years ago, I gained custody of Jordan, and he has lived with me ever since. However, that decision caused a deep rift. Because he chose to stay with me, the rest of the family, led by our mother, cut us off completely. We were denied all contact with our siblings, including Korin. After our mother passed away in 2019, the wall between us only grew higher, and I began to fear for what might be happening behind it.

But we never stopped praying. Every day, we reaffirm God's promise that He will restore what is broken. We envisioned them at home, laughing at the table, safe and healing. We declared it in faith, even when everything seemed hopeless.

Eventually, we learned the truth. Max and Korin were not okay. I went to court and obtained emergency orders to remove them from harm. We drove with a police escort to the house and woke them up—not for a visit, but to bring them home.

That moment was the answer to seven years of prayer. A miracle only God could have answered.

Tested by Fire, Crowned with Joy

After walking through fire after fire, I don't just believe God is good—I know it deep in my bones. That understanding didn't come easily. It was forged in pain, grief, panic, and miracles. But over time, suffering did something holy: it trained my soul to expect the goodness of God.

So, when the subsequent trial came, I didn't spiral out of control. I smiled.

In November, the mortgage company illegally foreclosed on the home I own and began eviction proceedings. The timing couldn't have been worse. I had just filed for bankruptcy. I had no savings. I have three children in wheelchairs, and both breeds are banned from most rentals. And a young woman we had taken in, a "stray," was living with us as a helper. In every way, the situation looked impossible.

But God.

Before my faith could even catch up, fear tried to take hold of me. But then my youngest daughter—the one who doesn't even believe in Jesus—looked at me and said, "Why aren't you excited? Don't you know great things are going to come out of this, like always?"

God used her words like a lightning bolt. I remembered who I was. Who's I was. I remembered the steps He taught me in the last fire—and I retook them right into this one.

<u>Step 1: Worship in the Middle</u>

Not after the breakthrough. Not once the paperwork clears. In the middle. That's when the real valuable things in life happen.

1. "I will bless the Lord at all times; His praise shall continually be in my mouth." – Psalm 34:1
2. "The Lord is my strength and my shield; my heart trusts in Him, and I am helped… and with my song, I will praise Him." – Psalm 28:7
3. "Though we live in the world, we do not wage war as the world does… The weapons we fight with… have divine power to demolish strongholds." – (2 Corinthians 10:3-5)
4. And don't forget—when God's people went to battle, the musicians went first. Not the warriors. (2 Chronicles 20:21-23)

So, I worshiped. Not because I felt like it. Because I knew it was the weapon.

<u>Step 2: Remember the Miracles</u>

I told my soul what God had already done. I rehearsed every supernatural provision, every door He kicked open, every "But God" moment that didn't make any sense naturally. And I reminded myself—I'm not starting from zero. He's already built a legacy of deliverance in my life.

1. "Remember the wonders he has done, his miracles, and the judgments He pronounced" –Psalm 105:6

2. "They overcame him by the blood of the Lamb and by the word of their testimony." – Revelation 12:11
3. "Bless the Lord, O my soul, and forget not all His benefits." – Psalm 103:2

Step 3: Be happy about Daily Manna

I didn't ask God for the whole plan—just the next step.

"God, what's my one act of obedience today?"

1. "Give us this day our daily bread." – Matthew 6:11
2. "With man this is impossible, but with God all things are possible." – Matthew 19:26
3. "Consider the lilies… they neither toil nor spin… will He not much more clothe you?" – (Matthew 6:28-33)

When God led His people through the desert, He gave them manna every day. But here's the part we forget, they weren't allowed to save it for tomorrow. If they hoarded it, it rotted. Why? Because He wanted them to wake up each day and trust Him again.

That's how I live now.

One Rhema at a time. One act of obedience at a time. One miracle at a time.

Just like the 12-step principle says: One. Day. At A. Time.

It's not a weakness. It's wisdom.

Step 4: Thank Him in Advance

Before I saw the outcome. Before I got a single phone call. I thanked God. Not because I had a reason, but because I had reasons. A whole history of them.

1. "Do not be anxious about anything, but in everything, by prayer and petition**, with thanksgiving**, present your requests to God." – Philippians 4:6

That kind of gratitude is prophetic. It speaks to the mountain before it moves. It doesn't wait for the storm to pass to start the celebration. It says, "You're the same God who showed up then—and You'll do it again." So I praised. I smiled. And when I told people what was happening, I was genuinely excited. People thought I was crazy. I was told to "live in reality" as if fear and stress were the correct response. And yes—it was Christians who said it. But I've learned that you don't follow their fear. You follow God's truth. And I'll tell you something wild: it wasn't even hard. I didn't have to fight to believe. There was no battle in my mind this time. No striving. Just joy. Just peace. Before I saw a single result.

And Then—God Moved

The mortgage company backed off for months. I didn't have to pay, which allowed me to save. When they pushed the eviction again, I praised it again. And now? They've backed off again. And on top of that, we're suing them. I went from nearly homeless… to staying in my home for free… to possibly receiving half a million dollars in damages. And you know what that means? It means we might finally be able to buy a bigger, wheelchair-accessible home. As I write this, we were just blessed with a brand-new 2024 wheelchair van—never used, worth $110,000! It all started two weeks ago when I called a place to see if they could fix Korin's chair. They told me they only sold wheelchair vans. I figured since I was already on the phone, I might as well ask about numbers. Two weeks later, we are picking up our brand-new van. Now, keep in mind—I just went bankrupt. Financing something like this should have been impossible. But God. Far Northern offered $44,000 toward the van, which the bank considered a substantial down payment. That opened the door to special financing. Not only did we get approved, but this financing will also help rebuild my credit, paving the way for me to buy a home in the future. It's like God dropped a booster rocket into my finances—a holy push forward to speed me toward

His promises because God is not limited by space, time, or bankruptcy court.

A Fire-Tested Faith

I share this not just to give God glory, but to invite you into this kind of faith. The kind that doesn't wait. The type that worships in ashes. The kind that throws a party in the middle of the storm because it knows who's in the boat.

God is still a God of miracles. And He is still a God of intimate, daily relationships. When we stand before Him, Scripture says everything we've done will be tested by fire, and only what we did with Him and for Him will remain. So I say: let the fire come. Let the world misunderstand me. Let the trials stack up. Because the suffering I've walked through has made me more loving, more surrendered, more whole, and more dangerous to the enemy. To the world, it may seem that I've accomplished a great deal. Like I've survived impossible things. But I know the truth. As Mother Teresa said, "I am just a pencil in the hand of God." And I'm so, so grateful that He could use this stubborn, mistake-filled, tender-hearted child of His to tell a story of faith.

God is always faithful. He is not done.

Chapter 3:

From Hustle to Holy Alignment: The Bold Identity Shift

Brehona Beverly

Have you ever chased success so hard that you lost sight of who you are and your God-given assignment?

I have.

And the truth is, it didn't happen overnight. It happened little by little, day by day, as I tried to be everything to everyone. I wasn't sinning. I was striving and not rebelling, just running. Trying to do what I thought would make God proud. What I thought would finally make everything "click."

Most days looked the same: the laptop was open, with numerous tabs, and audio training sessions buzzing in the background like white noise. I'm rocking my son to sleep, while racking my brain. I was torn. Not just between motherhood and business, but between who I knew I was and who I was trying so hard to be.

I'd wake up early, hoping the silence of the house would give me an edge before the day started. My baby would stir and then cry, but instead of greeting him with peace, I'd greet him with guilt about wanting a bit more free time to build my dream.

My body was there, but my mind was somewhere else. Absorbing courses. Downloading freebies. Listening to experts tell me, "This is the formula," "This is the strategy," "This is the secret." All while I felt like I was shrinking. Spiritually stagnant. Emotionally numb. Physically exhausted.

I believed I was building something for God. But I had forgotten how to rest and build with God.

And somewhere between downloading, strategizing, and overanalyzing, I started to feel like a machine. A spirit-led woman turned into a productivity app with a pulse. The dreams God gave me no longer felt sacred, they felt heavy. Not because they weren't from Him, but because I was trying to carry them in my strength.

The thoughts came in waves:

There has to be a way to break through.

There has to be a way.

I'd watch other women online, radiant, aligned, "successful, "and wonder how long it took them, and why I still hadn't cracked the code.

Maybe I need more knowledge, I'd tell myself.

More certifications. More validation. More… something.

But behind that hunger was fear.

Fear of failure.

Fear of being seen starting small.

Fear that maybe God didn't call me to this after all.

So I kept typing. Tinkering. Treading water in a sea of self-doubt, believing that if I could learn enough, I'd finally feel enough.

But I was consuming more than I was creating.

Planning more than I was praying.

Executing less than I was envisioning.

I was trying to build something holy on the blueprint of hustle.

You may know exactly what I mean. You love God. You pray. You fast. You dream big. And yet, there's still stagnation. A disconnect. A fatigue in your soul that can't be fixed with another podcast or planner.

If that's you, sis, this chapter is for you.

This isn't just a story about business burnout. It's a testimony of what happens when you lay down your hustle and pick up holy alignment. When you stop mimicking what worked for others and start co-creating with the Creator Himself.

Matthew 11:28 says, "Come to me, all you who are weary and burdened, and I will give you rest." It took rest and for me to bring all my business questions to the Lord, for me to see the breakthrough I desired.

This is the story of my Bold Identity Shift.

And it could be the beginning of yours.

Background

Before my Bold Identity Shift, I was doing all the "right" things but living all the wrong rhythms.

I was every coach's dream client. The one who showed up, took notes, bought the courses, joined the programs, downloaded the freebies, followed the gurus, and filled up iPhone notes and Google Docs with plans I never executed. I had an online library full of potential… and a heart full of pressure.

But underneath all that activity was a woman silently falling apart. A woman who loved God deeply but questioned if she had what it took. A woman battling with impostor syndrome disguised as "I just need to learn a little more."

I was hungry for clarity, but I was drowning in information. I was praying for confirmation but ignoring conviction. I was building, but not from intimacy. I was building from insecurity.

And then, I became a mother.

When my son was born, my world tilted. Everything I thought I had control over was suddenly on divine delay. Nap schedules replaced Zoom meetings. Feedings interrupted focus. I was no longer just managing time; I was being reshaped by it. I felt like I was disappearing into the background while the rest of the world kept launching and thriving without me.

But I didn't want to choose between the vision and my family, I wanted both. I wanted to build a business that gave me time freedom and flexibility, so I could be fully present with my son while also honoring the purpose God planted in my heart. I wanted to create a Kingdom legacy, not just a company, and show my son firsthand that you can do anything when you walk by faith with God.

To make that dream a reality, I joined a group coaching program and then a separate mastermind shortly after. I was determined. Motivated. Urgent. I wanted to make my business work.

But underneath that urgency was an ache—a growing exhaustion. I was being pulled in two directions: the purpose I carried and the pace that crushed me.

Even worse, comparison became my constant companion.

I'd scroll and see other women launching programs, speaking confidently on live video, glowing with success and clarity. And there I was, stuck in my robe with spit-up on my shoulder, wondering if I'd missed my window. Wondering if I was too late. Wondering if I even belonged.

I kept asking:

Should I pivot?

Do I even know enough?

Is this really God's plan, or am I just mimicking someone else's?

And while I waited for clarity to strike like lightning, I was avoiding the one thing that brings true clarity: obedience.

Before the shift, I was the queen of starting and stopping.

I'd sign up for a coaching program with the best of intentions, show up strong for the first few sessions, and then feel my spirit quietly pull back. "Build a challenge," they'd say. So, I tried. But something inside me resisted. It wasn't rebellion. It was misalignment.

I didn't want to build a challenge. It didn't fit the way God wired me to serve.

But instead of honoring that divine discomfort, I internalized it. I assumed I was the problem.

So, I joined another mastermind, thinking this time to "finish what I started." Surely more accountability would help. Surely this time I'd push through.

But again… I stalled.

Not because I was lazy. Not because I lacked vision. However, I was following strategies that didn't align with my spirit. I was mimicking someone else's method, hoping their success would somehow become mine.

Spoiler alert: it didn't.

Challenges work beautifully for many women. But for me? They felt heavy. Forced. Out of alignment. I'd launch with a smile but carry deep internal pressure. And still, I kept trying to twist myself into boxes God never built for me.

I also didn't realize at the time that I had become addicted to the high of a new beginning. The rush of a fresh idea. The illusion that this course, this coach, this launch would finally be the one.

But nothing stuck because none of it started from intimacy with God.

I was a woman of faith… but I was leading with fear.

Fear of failure.

Fear of what others would think.

Fear of missing out.

Fear of getting it wrong.

So, I lived in loops.

Overconsuming.

Under-executing.

Starting strong and stopping short.

Stuck in cycles of self-doubt, comparison, and perfectionism.

And it wasn't until I truly slowed down and invited God into the building with me that things began to shift.

I stopped praying for blueprints and started partnering in obedience.

I stopped copying and started listening.

I stopped chasing what looked successful and started creating what felt sacred.

I began hosting workshops and prayer gatherings that brought my spirit to life. I outsourced tasks that drained me, such as content planning, and focused on what filled me. I wasn't just doing business anymore. I was becoming someone new.

That's when I realized something that changed everything:

Breakthrough doesn't begin with strategy. It starts with identity.

God isn't just trying to help you build a brand.

He's trying to help you become who He always designed you to be.

The Turning Point

It didn't come with fanfare or fireworks. It came in the stillness. In the struggle. In a journal session that felt more like a wrestling match.

I remember sitting there, journal in hand, heart heavy. I was asking God again.

Am I really called to this? Coaching? Mentoring? Marketplace ministry?

I felt stagnant. I felt like I was stuck in spiritual quicksand.

No movement. No clarity. Just questions.

Do I even know enough? Can I really help someone with transformation? What if I'm not truly an expert? What if I mess it up?

My mind spun in circles. My heart ached under the weight of invisible pressure.

I wasn't just doubting the assignment, I was doubting myself.

I had been in a fog of information overload. I was "doing all the things," such as attending group coaching calls, filling Google Docs with notes, and signing up for masterminds to force myself into forward motion. But nothing stuck.

I kept building things I didn't want to build. Challenges. Programs. Funnels. All of which looked great on paper, but in reality drained me.

Every time I signed up for something new, I told myself, *This will be it. This will be the breakthrough.*

But instead of clarity, I felt heavy. Instead of momentum, I felt guilt. Because once again… I didn't follow through.

And still, I pressed on. Typing. Tinkering. Treading water in a sea of self-doubt and believing that if I could learn enough, I'd finally feel like enough.

But I wasn't just tired. I was weary.

That's when I poured it all out on paper. I stopped editing my prayers. I stopped pretending I was fine. I spilled the truth onto the page:

"God, I want to obey You… but am I really who You say I am?"

And right then, I heard it.

Clear. Quiet. Unmistakable.

"You're hustling to be seen when I've already called you chosen."

I understood the error of my ways. Tears welled up.

I realized I had been more focused on showing up like the world, than showing up like God sent me.

All that striving… all the endless planning and preparation… all the internal pressure to arrive, and all along, God had already affirmed me.

I had been scrambling to earn what I had already been given. Trying to validate a calling God had already confirmed.

I thought I had to be perfect to be effective.

That I had to have it all figured out before I could help anyone.

That I needed a platform, a program, a polished presence.

But God reminded me that He called me to serve women who are just a few steps behind me.

Women who love Him but are stuck in cycles of fear, procrastination, identity crisis, and performance.

Women who are over-consuming, under-executing, and quietly wondering if they're truly enough.

Women who want to honor God but are drowning in doubt.

And He whispered something more profound to my spirit:

You don't have to be the expert. You just have to be obedient.

That day didn't fix everything. But it broke something:

The lie that I had to be someone else to be effective.

The lie that my voice wasn't powerful unless it sounded like hers.

The lie that God needed me to be polished when all He wanted was my yes.

He showed me that my wilderness wasn't wasted.

That every season of confusion, every stretch of silence, every tear and detour and delay had been part of His training ground.

And then He reminded me:

I've given you everything you need. My Spirit. My Word. My presence. You are already equipped. You are not disqualified. You are not too late. And you are not alone.

All I had to do was show up.

He would meet me there.

He would fill my mouth.

He would move through my obedience.

That was the moment everything shifted.

The moment I stopped hustling to be seen…

And started walking in the truth that I was already chosen.

The Shift: Birth of the B.O.L.D. Framework

The B.O.L.D. Identity Shift Framework was developed in the valley.

It came together piece by piece through breakdowns, breakthroughs, and a thousand whispered prayers.

Not from a course or a mastermind, but from the quiet, raw, and sacred spaces where God met me in my confusion, in my questions, and in my obedience.

Over time, as I reflected on my patterns, including my starting and stopping, my fear, and my striving, I saw a thread running through all of it: an identity crisis.

Not a branding issue. Not a niche issue.

An identity issue.

I didn't believe I was already enough in Christ. I believed I had to earn it.

I believed I had to be more polished, more experienced, more knowledgeable before I could fully own my calling.

I didn't feel like an expert; instead, I felt like a woman with a heart full of purpose and fear.

After months of confusion, stagnation, and false starts, I realized that the root of my struggle wasn't a lack of knowledge or strategy.

It was a lack of security in who God said I was.

When I became honest about my fears of failure, fear of man, and fear of getting it wrong, I began to see just how much they had ruled my decisions.

It had made me shrink.

It had made me stall.

It had made me seek approval more than alignment.

But when I reclaimed my identity as a daughter of the King, when I remembered that God hasn't given me a spirit of fear but of power, love, and a sound mind, everything began to shift.

That's when the framework came to life.

Not all at once.

But in layers.

In lessons.

In journal entries and spirit-led nudges.

In failed launches and gentle reminders.

In stillness, not striving.

It didn't come out of thin air, it grew through my surrender.

And from that lived transformation, the B.O.L.D. Identity Shift Framework was born.

Not as a business tool, but as a lifeline.

A Spirit-led path back to the woman God originally designed me to be.

A way to trade fear for faith.

To move from striving to surrender.

To step into purpose with clarity, confidence, and Christ at the center.

The B stands for 'Break Free'

I had to stop trying to earn what God had already freely given. I had to let go of the lies and limiting beliefs that told me I wasn't enough. And when I did, I found freedom.

I had to break free before I could build. Break free from what? From fear. From perfectionism. From overthinking and overconsumption. From comparison, that had me studying other people's lanes while I ignored my own.

For years, I confused preparation with progress. I spent so much time getting ready to get ready, from perfecting outlines and tweaking my messaging to bingeing on courses and content. I didn't realize that the longer I stayed stuck in the consumption cycle, the more I was avoiding the obedience God was calling me to.

I remember one night specifically. The house was quiet, the baby asleep, the browser open with four tabs of coaching content from other leaders I admired. But instead of feeling inspired, I felt paralyzed. I wasn't moving forward. I was mimicking. Copying. Trying to imitate other coaches' strategies, offers, and voice.

That night, God spoke gently but firmly: "I didn't call you to build like her. I called you to be you."

I realized I had been so busy trying to sound like everyone else that I couldn't even recognize my own voice anymore. I had abandoned the unique sound God placed inside me, the one designed to awaken my people.

That was the beginning of my freedom.

Freedom came with every small act of obedience. Every time I turned off a podcast to sit in silence with God. Every time I deleted a saved post, I asked the Holy Spirit instead. Every time I started asking, "God, what are You saying?"

And the more I broke free from those mindsets, the more I began to hear again. To create again. To move in faith, even if I was afraid.

It turns out that breaking free wasn't about cutting off the world. It was about connecting more deeply with God, which changed everything.

Proverbs 29:25 says, 'The fear of man lays a snare, but whoever trusts in the Lord is safe.' Fear of man and the fear of failure kept me stuck and stagnant. Trusting and inquiring of the Lord caused me to build in peace and alignment.

The O stands for 'Own Your Calling'

This one was the scariest. It meant stepping up before I felt "ready." It meant coaching, leading, and mentoring before I had a polished brand or viral content. It meant saying, "Yes, Lord, send me," even when I questioned my qualifications. It meant speaking up, showing up, and not shrinking back.

Owning my calling out loud was the shift that scared me the most.

It's one thing to think you're called. It's another thing entirely to declare it. To live it. To build around it. To be responsible for the weight of it.

For a long time, I waited for external validation, for someone to affirm what God had already revealed. I kept asking, "Who am I to lead women in their faith journey? Who am I to coach someone when I still have questions of my own?"

But here's what I learned: God doesn't call the qualified, He qualifies the called. And when He whispered, "You are called to mentor, to teach, to disciple," it wasn't a suggestion. It was a charge.

Still, I wrestled.

What if I get it wrong? What if I don't have enough experience? What if someone challenges my authority?

God met every question with the same answer: "I called you."

I had to start saying it out loud before I felt "ready." I had to introduce myself as a Kingdom coach, a faith mentor, and a guide for women stepping into purpose. I had to walk into digital and physical rooms with the conviction that I belonged there, not because of me, but because of the One who sent me.

I began to notice something: every time I spoke up in obedience, clarity followed. Every time I took action, confidence grew.

I remember one specific coaching call with a woman who was grieving a significant life transition. I felt unqualified, but I showed up anyway. As I spoke, prayed, and guided her through the Word, the atmosphere shifted. She cried. I cried. She left with peace and purpose, and I left knowing, "This is who I am. This is what I was made to do."

Owning your calling doesn't start when you feel ready. It begins when you decide to believe God.

And that decision? It will change everything and create momentum.

Jeremiah 1:5 says, 'Before I formed you in the womb I knew you, and before you were born I consecrated you.' God chose and appointed me before I was conceived, and it was time to live like it.

The L stands for 'Live in Alignment'

Alignment is not about imitation. It's about intimacy. I had to stop building someone else's vision and start asking God, "What are You building with me today?" I stopped chasing someone else's lane and embraced the one God assigned to me. That's when things started to flow.

Living in alignment meant unlearning everything the world told me I needed to do to be successful, and tuning in to who God was asking me to become.

It meant building from a different blueprint. Not the one I downloaded or studied. The one God whispered in the secret place.

For so long, I was addicted to strategy. I believed if I just found the right method, the perfect funnel, the highest-converting script, then everything would fall into place. But what I lacked wasn't strategy, it was surrender.

True alignment came when I started partnering with God moment by moment.

Instead of planning first and praying second, I flipped it. I started asking, "Lord, what are we doing today?" I let Him shape my schedule. I let Him prioritize my to-do list. And I stopped forcing things that felt heavy, even if they looked "right."

One of the most significant signs of alignment is peace. Not ease, but peace. When I'm aligned with what God is doing in and through me, I feel it in my spirit. There's grace on it. It flows.

I recall a time when I was preparing content and hit a block. Nothing I wrote felt inspired. It all felt forced. So, I stopped. I shut the laptop, walked away, and sat in silence. After praying for a few minutes, the Holy Spirit began speaking. The message I was trying to write on my own started pouring out from God's heart. That content became one of my most impactful teachings because it was God inspired.

Alignment doesn't just change your content, it increases your confidence.

You no longer need to chase trends because you're anchored in truth. You don't have to mimic others because you're finally at peace with who you are.

Alignment doesn't guarantee overnight success. But it does ensure that you'll build something that lasts.

The D stands for 'Do It Afraid'

Courage isn't the absence of fear, it's obedience despite it. I went live without my hair being pressed, launched programs without landing pages, and sent direct messages despite my nerves. I hosted workshops for four women, and I poured into one woman as if she were a crowd. I learned that God honors movement, not mastery.

If I had waited to feel fearless, I'd still be waiting.

"Do it afraid" became my mantra in the seasons when my heart was pounding, my hands were trembling, and my voice felt too small. But here's what I've learned: God doesn't require perfection. He requires obedience.

I've gone live on social media with no script, no makeup, and no plan, just a word from the Lord and a shaky yes. Sometimes the message flowed. Other times I stumbled over my words, ended the live, took a deep breath, and tried again.

I've hosted workshops with only one or two women present. At first, I felt like a failure. But then God reminded me: "If I can trust you with one, I can trust you with many." So I poured into them as if the room were full because Heaven celebrates faithfulness, not followers.

I've prayed with women over Zoom, stayed hours after scheduled sessions just to encourage a sister who needed someone to believe with her. I've sent cold messages to women I hadn't spoken to in years, sharing my story, offering support, and trusting that even if they didn't respond, the seed was still sown.

None of it felt glamorous. But every act of obedience released something in the Spirit.

My courage didn't come from rehearsing or polishing. It came from moving. And every time I did it, afraid, God met me. Every time I showed up, He showed out.

Fear is not a reason to pause. It's a signal to press in. Because what's on the other side of fear is freedom, not just for you, but for those assigned to your voice.

So show up. Even trembling. Even unsure. Even in tears.

Because when you move, God moves with you.

The B.O.L.D. Identity Shift Framework came from consecration. And every time I walk another woman through it, I watch God breathe on her life, her voice, and her calling in a way that only He can.

Transformation Testimony: The Fruit of Obedience

I've learned that obedience doesn't just change me, it activates change in others.

One of the most sacred parts of my calling has been creating safe, Spirit-filled spaces where women can finally breathe. Cry. Be vulnerable. Be seen.

I've sat with women who were grieving, not just losses, but identity. Women who no longer knew who they were. Who questioned if God still had a plan for them. Who felt like they were walking through a wilderness with no direction.

And God would meet us there.

Through simple conversations. Through prayer. Through sacred silence and Holy Spirit-led words, women have found space to release from frustration, disappointment, and shame, to remember who they are.

I've watched women who once felt stuck in fear start to speak with clarity and confidence.

I've seen women who were paralyzed by overthinking begin to take bold, faith-filled action.

I've witnessed women who had drifted from God's presence return to intimacy, prayer, and power, not through pressure, but through the presence of God.

We've opened the Word together.

We've prayed for healing and deliverance together.

We've prophesied life over dead dreams, dead marriages, dead confidence.

And we've reminded each other: God is not finished. He's just getting started.

Through my coaching and community, I've helped women:

- Transition through grief and identity loss by anchoring them in truth.
- Move from confusion to clarity in their purpose and calling.
- Build boldness through repeated small steps of obedience.
- Deepen intimacy with God through journaling, prayer, and Word-based routines.
- Detach from striving and rest in the grace and strength of the Holy Spirit.

And what's emerged isn't just better business strategies, it's transformed daughters.

Women are walking in authority now.

Speaking life over themselves.

Claiming their position as Kingdom ambassadors.

Knowing they are fearfully and wonderfully made.

Believing they are called, appointed, chosen, and anointed for such a time as this.

They are no longer waiting to be picked. They are owning their seat at the table God prepared.

Because we are not just called to impact, we are called to inherit.

We are the royal priesthood.

The salt. The light. The glory carriers.

Mothers, entrepreneurs, ministers, makers of change.

Daughters of the Most High God, called to walk in wholeness, in joy, in peace, and power.

That's the fruit of saying yes to God.

That's the legacy of holy alignment.

And it is only just beginning.

Ephesians 3:20 says, 'Now to Him who is able to do exceedingly abundantly above all that we ask or think, according to the power that works in us…" Saying yes to God creates a life of purpose and abundance that we haven't even asked for or dreamed of.

Living in Abundance

Today, I don't just wake up earlier, I wake up lighter.

There's still responsibility. There's still a business to run, a family to care for, and dreams to steward. But now? I wake up with peace, not pressure. I plan from a place of presence, not performance. I operate from alignment, not anxiety.

Because I've learned something life-changing:

Followers, funnels, or finances don't measure true abundance.

True abundance is alignment.

Today, my life and business feel different. Not because everything is perfect, but because everything is purposeful.

There's more peace.

More joy.

More trust.

I no longer wake up with pressure clawing at my chest or a to-do list that feels like a ticking bomb. I wake up with gratitude. With intimacy. With a quiet assurance that God is perfecting everything that concerns me, even the things I can't yet see.

I know now that He is the One who makes my path straight.

He opens doors I didn't know existed.

He orchestrates divine connections and quiet miracles behind the scenes.

I don't have to chase strategy, I follow His Spirit.

I don't treat God like a silent business partner. I treat Him like the CEO, the mentor, the friend.

I walk with Him. I talk to Him. I include Him in the day-to-day details, just like I would my son, my husband, or my community.

"God, what are we doing today?"

"Can I take this next step?"

"Do You want me to say this?"

Those aren't rhetorical questions anymore. They're real-time conversations.

And He responds. His Spirit speaks. His love ministers. His guidance sharpens.

I don't move without Him. I check in with Him like I check in with my calendar.

This isn't hyper-spiritual. It's holy-normal.

It's how Kingdom daughters do life.

Now, my life flows differently.

I've grown spiritually in ways I can't always put into words. I hear His voice more clearly. I sense His peace more quickly. I recover from fear more gracefully. I walk with a deeper level of trust, knowing that my Father wrote the end from the beginning, and the victory is already mine in Christ Jesus.

Psalm 16:11 says: "You make known to me the path of life; in Your presence there is fullness of joy; at Your right hand are pleasures forevermore."

That's exactly what I've found, joy, not just in big wins, but in ordinary moments.

I've surrounded myself with a community of like-minded women who love God, lead with integrity, and do life together with vulnerability and faith.

I'm not building alone anymore, and I'm no longer building just for impact.

I'm building for eternity.

In business, I no longer scramble to post what's trending. I speak what's true.

I don't obsess overreach; I focus on relevance.

I know that the women God has called me to serve will hear my voice, and when they do, they'll awaken.

My spiritual maturity has deepened because I no longer compartmentalize God; I commune with Him.

And in that communion, I've discovered the trustworthy source of abundance.

It's not just about clarity in business, it's clarity in identity.

It's confidence rooted in truth.

It's courage that grows through obedience.

Now, when I act in faith, my confidence increases.

My self-doubt fades.

My courage strengthens.

Why?

Because I know who I am. And I know whose I am.

Without that identity in Christ, nothing ever felt good enough.

I never felt good enough.

But now?

Now, I know I'm already loved. Already chosen. Already equipped.

I no longer mimic others' blueprints. God gave me my own lane. My own strategy. My own people to serve. And when I show up in obedience, the right women hear me, and they begin to awaken, blossom, and break free too.

This is what abundance looks like.

Not striving, but stewarding.

Not chasing success, but embodying significance.

Not hustling to be seen, but walking as someone already chosen.

Encouragement

Sis, I know it's hard.

I know what it's like to feel stuck, not because you don't care, but because you care so much.

You want to get it right. You want to honor God. You want to steward the dream He's placed inside of you.

But all that wanting has turned into waiting.

Waiting for clarity.

Waiting for confidence.

Waiting for confirmation.

And in the waiting, you've started to question yourself:

Am I really enough? Did God really call me? What if I fail?

Let me remind you of something foundational: even your salvation started with faith.

Faith that Jesus lived, died, rose again, and now reigns victorious at the right hand of the Father.

It all began with believing.

And the same faith that saved you… will also sustain you.

Hebrews 11:6 reminds us, "Without faith, it is impossible to please God."

But with faith comes trust.

And if your heart is heavy and your path feels unclear, this is your moment to trust Him deeper.

Trust that He's working it all out behind the scenes.

Trust that He's not punishing you, He's positioning you.

Trust that He has plans for you. Beautiful. Sovereign. Divine.

God is not a man that He should lie.

His mercy is new every morning.

His love for you is unshakable.

And He has a covenant with you that He will not break.

Faith is not just belief; it's a movement.

It's action in the face of fear.

It's saying yes before you see the full staircase.

It's trusting God enough to obey when all you have is a whisper.

You're not stuck because you're lazy.

You're stuck because you're scared.

And that's okay, but it's not where your story ends.

You don't need another strategy.

You need to surrender.

You don't need a platform.

You need presence.

You don't need to be perfect.

You just need to say yes.

Because as you move, clarity will come.

Peace will rise.

Revelation will meet you.

And God will show you where to pivot, how to adjust, and what step to take next.

Your obedience opens the door to divine alignment.

So, trust Him. Trust the Father who sees you.

Who knows you.

Who has never failed you.

Who called you before the foundation of the world and equipped you with everything you need.

You are not too late.

You are not disqualified.

You are not falling behind.

You are being built.

Your identity fuels your destiny.

And your next step, no matter how small, is sacred.

Proverbs 3:5–6 says: "Trust in the Lord with all your heart and lean not on your own understanding; in all your ways acknowledge Him, and He shall direct your paths."

So walk with boldness.

Walk with faith.

Walk like the daughter of the King that you are.

Say yes again, not because you have it all figured out, but because God already does.

I see you.

I believe in you.

And more importantly, God sees you.

He loves you.

And He's waiting for your yes.

So go ahead:

Do it afraid.

Do it anyway.

Do it with God.

And watch Him do what only He can do.

Reflection Prompts

2. Where in my life or business have I been striving more than surrendering? What would it look like to invite God into that space today?
3. When was the last time I questioned my calling?
4. Write down what the voice of fear has been telling you, and then ask God what He says instead.

5. Which part of the B.O.L.D. framework do I feel most called to focus on right now?
6. Break Free. Own Your Calling. Live in Alignment. Do It Afraid.
7. What does abundance look like for me?
8. Ask God to redefine abundance in your life today. Write down what He shows you.
9. Who in my life could experience a breakthrough if I showed up in obedience?
10. What's the next small step God is asking me to take?

Prayer of Activation

Father God,

Thank You for every daughter who reads these words.

Thank You that You see her, not just for what she does, but for who she is: chosen, loved, equipped, and called.

Right now, I lift up every fear, every delay, every lie she's believed about not being enough.

I break agreement with the spirit of striving, and I speak supernatural alignment over her life.

Let her identity in You become louder than every doubt in her head.

Holy Spirit, awaken the boldness within her.

Give her courage to break free from comparison, to own her unique calling, to walk in alignment with Heaven's rhythm, and to move even when she's afraid.

Let this not just be a chapter she reads, but a chapter she lives.

May she rise in authority. Speak with confidence. Lead with love. And co-create with the Creator who never leaves her side.

Lord, I release divine strategy, Kingdom community, and peace that passes understanding over her life.

Let her know that her YES still matters and that it's never too late to partner with You.

In Jesus' name,

Amen.

Declarations for Bold Faith & Divine Alignment

- I am chosen by God and called for such a time as this.
- I have everything I need to serve, lead, and build with boldness.
- I will no longer shrink; I rise in confidence and walk in my Kingdom authority.
- I break the agreement with fear, doubt, and perfectionism.
- I trust the Holy Spirit to guide, instruct, and equip me every step of the way.
- I am not behind, I am being built by God, on His perfect timeline.
- I let go of striving and step into alignment with God's pace and presence.
- I do not copy because I am a divine original with a Heaven-breathed blueprint.
- I choose faith over fear. Movement over perfection. Obedience over overthinking.

- I declare that I am a daughter of the King, anointed, appointed, and empowered.
- My words carry life. My presence shifts atmospheres. My obedience births legacy.
- I build with God, not just for Him. And I trust that He is leading me every step of the way.
- My purpose is bigger than a platform, it is eternal, and it will not be delayed.
- I declare supernatural clarity, divine strategy, and boldness to move forward.
- I say YES again. Not because I have it all figured out, but because God already does.

Chapter 4:

When It's Time To Turn The Page

Stacey E. Campbell

"I AM THE TIDE"

This is a daily affirmation for the women who give everything, and is now giving herself back (speak aloud, journal it, or simply breathe it in)

I am the TIDE-ever-flowing, ever-knowing. I rise and I retreat, with purpose and power.

I have drifted through exhaustion, crashed against the cliffs of overgiving.

But I am still here, still sacred, still sovereign.

I no longer confuse burnout with bravery. I do not need to break myself to prove myself.

My worth is not in my output, but in my being.

I give myself permission to rest without apology.

To say no without explanation. To choose me without guilt.

The balance I seek is not perfection. It is present.

A rhythm that honors my body, my mind, and my joy.

My work is important. But so is my well-being. So is my breath. So is my peace.

I will not shrink to fit old roles. I will not bend to meet expectations that betray me.

I walk forward in alignment, not in overextension. I am not behind. I am becoming.

And this season, it's not survival-it's restoration. I embrace the light

And I am allowed to shine without burning out

As I look back on my chapter Becoming a Rose without the Thorns, in the Living In Her Abundance On Purpose: Chosen For Such a Time as This Anthology, my journey towards Grief and Loss was not complete. Although I finished the chapter work, deep down, I still have work to do.

I have come to realize that my history is marked by pain, resilience, and a journey of growth that many can relate to. As I have previously written, the time to turn the page toward happiness, self-care, and aligning my life with my goals is now, as I have already begun the process.

Let me explain why:

I have found my voice. I wrote the previous chapter, which was not just about telling my story; I had to own it. I am no longer hiding behind, "I can't go and tell people my business." I have stepped into the light. That moment of saying "My motivation is: ME" was my declaration that the healing had begun—and that I was ready to prioritize myself.

I have experienced profound grief. I have endured significant loss and have carried its weight for thirty-six years. However, being able to tell my story without breaking and to reflect and share shows that I have processed enough to move on. I have honored my past—now it's time to honor my future.

I am already blooming. The metaphor of becoming a ROSE Without the Thorns is powerful. It doesn't mean forgetting the pain; it means I have survived the thorns, and now I am allowing myself to flourish. I recognize my value, beauty, and purpose—even if it has taken years. That is blooming. That is becoming.

I am ready to align my external life with my internal growth. I am no longer satisfied with just surviving—I want to thrive, in every area of my life. The fact is a shift that is already happening in my mind and heart. The seed has already been planted, now I need to help it grow strong and steady, one page at a time.

There comes a time in life when the heart and the head don't always agree—and I find myself at these crossroads both professionally and personally. For years, I dedicated myself to the demanding world of home health and hospice. It was a field I deeply respected, one that challenged me and gave me a sense of purpose. The fast-paced environment, emotional intensity, and sense of urgency became familiar territory. It was stressful, competitive, and often overwhelming—but there was also something profoundly fulfilling about being part of someone's care during such a vulnerable time.

I recall thinking many times how people sit around and let the days slip away. Then, one day, they look up and realize it's been one, two, or even three years—and they wonder where the time went. Every second becomes a minute, every minute an hour, every hour a day, every day a week, every week a month, and every month a year. That thought started to weigh heavily on me. I understood that if I didn't start making changes, I might end up wondering where my own time had gone—and why I hadn't listened to that quiet voice urging me to align my life and make some choices.

My professional crossroads came when I was at work one day, laughing and talking with my coworker as we discussed our daily work plans, and I looked up to notice that everyone was almost younger than I was. But what was new? It is life, and someone will always be younger or older than you.

Later that day, I attended a professional networking event and took another look around. I was one of the older people in the room. As I drove home, I thought to myself, "Girl, you are amazing." I reflected on my age, personality, self-worth, knowledge, drive, grit, reliability, and other parts of myself. I realized I am still dominating the game, not just by 10, 15, or 20 years, but over 30 years older than some of the people I network with and work with.

During an evening chat with my family, I shared my day and thoughts with them. I explained what life is like for a salesperson and how it can be exhausting always keeping track of what A, B, and C are doing, watch for competitors entering the area, stay on top of policies, worry if someone received the proper care, and wonder if I reached my daily and monthly goals.

They assured me that I am skilled at what I do. I continued to explain that, like others, they did not experience the low and high peak moments, nor the stressful times. They mostly saw happy, fun, and celebratory moments. They saw the celebrations but not the stress. In sales, you never get to exhale fully. Each new month resets the pressure, the drive, and the chase. And while the rewards are real—both emotional and financial—the demands are relentless.

These are moments that last the entire month. When someone is in sales, they rarely have time to breathe, even if they're on top. Someone is always chasing the top spot. We stress out and hold our breath to meet our goals, and when the month ends, we wake up, only to start all over again the next day. Month after month, this is the sales cycle. But the adrenaline rush is addictive. Not to mention how all that hard work results in hard-earned commissions. That was a conversation that came and went.

As days went by, I kept asking myself, Where will I be five years from now? I panicked when I realized I would be 62. Am I saving enough for retirement? How is my health now, and how will it be in five years? I started pulling Social Security and 401(k) information and thinking about when I could retire based on that data. As I reviewed everything, I thought, "HELL NO," I didn't want to retire at that age. My mind was racing with thoughts about my conversations with myself, and I had to ask, Do I want to be close to the age my mother was when she passed? She died at 71. That would mean I'd only have a few years to enjoy my life.

Working in healthcare requires constant availability. Not all holidays feel like holidays. Balancing schedules can be challenging at times. It's difficult to stop thinking about those who need help during challenging moments.

I kept questioning myself: Do I still want to keep pounding the pavement day in and day out in the sales field? Do I want to give up the connections, friendships, events, highs, lows, and so on? I think of all the people I have helped over the years with services, including patients and professional connections, as this is where I strive and thrive. The outcomes I create are what keep me at the top of my game and connected.

Therefore, I answered my own question. No, I did not want to stop doing what I love. Nothing was broken, so why change it? I was living a happy work life day after day. I was content and complacent. But was I truly fulfilled?

As meaningful as the work was, it wasn't the path I had imagined for myself. My heart has always been pulled toward empowering others to live fuller lives through advocacy, support, and education. I value and respect every relationship and each person I encounter. As we all know, being kind and respectful to others can lead to positive outcomes.

One day, out of nowhere, I received a text message from a friend asking how things were going. She said that she had been thinking about me and would love to meet for lunch. I didn't think much of it because we often met socially. However, before that lunch happened, she reached out to tell me she was leaving her current job. My heart immediately sank, and I felt broken for the job and organization she worked for because she was the face of both.

She proceeded to tell me that she was looking to advance her career and achieve her future goals. Then, she expressed that she would love for me to consider applying for the position she was vacating. I am very familiar with the organization she worked for and have always admired its values. Recently, I have written multiple papers in college about this organization, modeling my assignments after it and using it as an example.

The first thing I thought was 'thank you, but no thank you,' because I was very happy where I was and loved what I was doing. There was nothing wrong, so why change? I thought. However, since I valued her opinion, friendship, and believed in the organization, we continued with plans to meet for lunch, conversation, and socialization.

During our lunch, we shared both professional and personal conversations, and I admired the balance she showed. As a result, I left feeling more confused because I realized this was the balance I needed in my life at this moment, and the position would suit me well.

That evening, I went home and discussed the phone call I had with my family; they reacted the same way I did. I had been at my current job for barely a year, everything was going well, and I was happy. So once again... why change?

In defense of considering the upcoming job position I mentioned, I highlighted all the great benefits, retirement packages, and opportunities I'd have working with various nationwide organizations rather than local accounts. I would still stay connected to the community I knew so well. Honestly, I had always looked at open positions at this organization to match my needs and goals. Still, there was never anything compatible enough to be as fulfilling as my current role. Then I thought about the balance and what the organization and position represented. Once again, I thought, 'Why change?'

Over the days, I reviewed the job position on paper, online, and through other means, looking for anything negative. But I found none. I knew other people who worked there and used this organization as a resource. It was my account I had called on for sales calls year after year, regardless of which organization I was with or what role I held. I felt conflicted. I have always advised others to find their balance and happiness, but I rarely follow my own advice.

Because I am driven by adrenaline and live by deadlines, I knew I had a down-to-the-wire moment to submit my cover letter and resume. Truth be told, I did not want to make the mistake of submitting the information, and if I changed my mind and rescinded my application, I did not want to appear unreliable. At the same time, I thought, "What if I did not take the opportunity and apply, and someone else got the position?" Couldn't have that happen, now, could I?

However, I kept taking my time sending out my cover letter and resume. My good friend, who had referred me, texted me every other day. Finally, she sent a message saying that if I needed help applying or updating my information, she was there to assist. That wasn't the case, as I always keep my employment info current. As I mentioned earlier, I was uncertain and conflicted, and deep down, I felt that this would be my next job transition.

The uncertainty mentioned above stemmed from knowing that I would be transitioning from sales and marketing to outreach and education, which also meant giving up a commissioned position. Commission is something that I have grinded for, for years. It has guided me in reaching my goals and measuring my success.

I applied the day before the announcement closed. My friend sent me a text complimenting my cover letter and telling me how strong it was. I responded to her, letting her know that whatever the case may be, I had to stand out and above my competition for the position.

When I received an email for a job interview, I knew things were about to get real. I barely knew a few of the interviewers, and I understood I had to do what I do best. I had to sell myself. I had to outperform the competition. Deep down, I felt that this job was meant for me. I was familiar with the organization's history through research I completed for a class assignment, as well as through my interactions with employees there and my ongoing relationship with the organization. I was able to confidently walk into that interview with a clear plan to secure the job.

That night, while cleaning out a work bin, I found multiple signs that the job was meant for me. I came across pens, bookmarks, books, and various marketing materials from the organization. The last bin I emptied contained a self-care journal with their logo on it. As I glanced through the journal and the words within it, I knew this job was for me.

Two days later, I received the call: I had been chosen for the position. I proudly and immediately accepted, but I was torn. I panicked because I thought about all the relationships and friendships I had built over the years based on my previous job roles. Then I weighed the pros and cons of my current salary versus the potential future salary. As a salesperson, I thrive on commission, and I knew that if I moved forward, I would lose that source of income. I reached out to a few family members and trusted individuals, and all of them unanimously told me to consider the benefits I would gain for my future.

It was easier for me to tell my family than it was to tell my current employer. I didn't want to let my work team down or appear as though I was abandoning ship. But deep down, I knew I needed to find somewhere else.

My family gave me many reasons not to make that change. I remember my daughter sat next to me and said that at my current job, it was the first time in a long while she had seen me not stressed. She said I seemed to enjoy my work life and didn't come home with negative energy or complaints about my day. She didn't realize, deep down, I was tired of the daily grind and hustle, and I needed a different professional path, outlook, and outcome.

I sternly told her that it was time for me to take a job for myself, not for the good of the household. It felt like a dark cloud had appeared, as uncertainty prevailed among the family about the household's future.

I extended the start date twice to ensure I didn't leave the job and the team I worked closely with in a situation where my duties were not yet complete. My name and phone number were linked to and attached to events that had already been planned. I also missed out on receiving one-on-one training for the position because my friend had already started her new job.

Leaving the home health and hospice world was a bittersweet choice. I let go of a role that once felt like my purpose. However, by doing so, I discovered a different kind of purpose that honors my original dreams, supports my well-being, and provides me with space to grow in new ways. The pace is manageable, the stress is less overwhelming, and the mission remains meaningful.

Therefore, I chose to turn the page. PROFESSIONALLY!!!

Turning the page at a personal crossroads can be stressful, but it can also bring wisdom, acceptance, experience, and emotional maturity.

As I start to embrace my age professionally, I am doing the same personally. I have to acknowledge that nothing remains the same forever. This realization is awakening.

Not only am I emotionally maturing, but my daughter is also growing into a very responsible and focused young woman. She is driven, busy, outgoing, dependable, goal-oriented, and more. Watching her live her 22-year-old life brings me joy, as she comes into her own with such confidence.

Each day as I watch her, I see myself at her age. Our interests may differ, but our passion and zest for life are the same. Our household is always busy. This busyness includes, and continues to include, family dinners, holidays, parties, and dance. It resembles the busy life I grew up with as a child, although sports have replaced dance. I was involved in cheerleading, the debate team, 4-H, and took guitar and piano lessons, as well as participating in basketball, volleyball, track, softball, and attending two different churches. I am sure I am missing more. It was jam-packed, fun, and my normal.

I watched my grandmother's and mother's health decline as they set their self-care aside, prioritizing others' needs over their own. I've been doing the same—putting others' needs before mine. A good friend of mine and I often remind each other by asking, if you were on a plane, who would you put the mask on first? Yourself.

I was speaking with a friend one day, and he commented that he wished he had a life like mine because I seemed to have a fun life, always doing something or going somewhere. Not realizing that there were three parties, I committed to attending that day, and they were causing me a bit of stress and anxiety as I had to calculate how much time I could spend at each party so that I wouldn't be late for the others, and that didn't include driving time.

I made it to each party as planned, and everything went flawlessly. My daughter was with me for two of the parties I attended, and once again, I thought, even though she is 36 years younger than I, I can keep up, and that made me proud of myself.

That pride, however, caused me severe exhaustion the next day. I woke up and thought about how it hadn't been an enjoyable evening, as I was overwhelmed and unable to fully enjoy the good company and meaningful conversations. I had depleted my emotional, mental, and physical reserves. Although I am an extrovert, I experienced burnout and imbalance, and stayed in bed for the rest of that day. I felt a loss of inner alignment. Let's face it, many of us don't bounce back as easily as we once did.

I decided to reach out to my employer's One Health Program and requested a Zoom call with a Wellness and Balance Life Coach. That one telehealth visit opened my eyes and made me realize I need to realign my priorities. As I shared my life with this professional, I overloaded her with so much information about my life and activities that she told me she couldn't even set a goal for me to focus on. Instead, she asked me to review what I had told her, sign off on it, and we would check back in the next week. I dismissed the next appointment, and it took me months to revisit the notes she had sent me.

As I read the notes one morning before I went to work, I cried. They were not what I had expected. I noted that I was all over the place and thought, How have I been keeping up with life? I kept up with everything and everyone but myself. I was going through life as what I thought was normal. By living a fast-paced life, I had given myself little time to process, reflect, and recover. There had been no off switch; my mode was always stuck in the on position.

Later that day, while I was at work, I received a call from my daughter, and she was crying on the other end. She said she had just left the counselor's office at school and wouldn't be graduating until the next semester because she still needed to complete other classes. She had recently changed her major and had to start a new educational path. She was confused because she had done what her counselor instructed her to do and was carrying the 15 units as suggested. She was working, choreographing, interning as an athletic trainer, and still trying to be a 22-year-old. I felt helpless because all I could do was tell her to take a couple of deep breaths, calm down, wipe away her tears, and go to her other classes, even though it would be hard. We agreed to talk about this situation that evening. I felt overwhelmed, especially since I had cried tears that very morning over my own well-being struggles, and now I was absorbing my daughter's tears and confusion. It was such a draining and emotional experience! As a parent, I was always ready to fix her problems, hurt, issues, and pain. But when I became a Life Coach, I explained to her that I was there to help her reach her goals through support, guidance, and suggestions.

When I got home that evening, I was surprised to find her calm, as I had expected to walk into emotional chaos. She informed me that during class, her instructor commented that her spirits seemed down, and she recounted what had just happened with the counselor. Her instructor mentioned that she had recently heard of a couple of similar situations with other students, and she planned to contact the athletic department's counselor and told her to reach out as well. She did so and had an appointment the next day.

She came home hopeful, her voice and eyes shining. She told me how the athletic counselor was surprised by the educational path she was told to take to graduate. He said he would contact her in a few days and was working on a way to make it possible for her to walk the stage.

She called me exactly two days after the athletic counselor said he would contact her to share the good news. He was able to rearrange classes so that credits and grades were assigned correctly. However, it still depended on her passing each class she was enrolled in. This caused some anxiety, but she studied and turned in extra credit assignments to ensure there was plenty of room for adjustments if any other issues arose.

She was overwhelmed with cognitive overload, burnout, and emotional depletion. She couldn't focus on the joy and happiness of her upcoming college graduation. After a few disagreements about whether to have a graduation party, I respected her decision. I took a moment to notice that she was trying to get through everything so she could celebrate her win.

At that moment, I let go and realized that she was in charge of and responsible for her outcome. We decided to abandon the idea of planning a party and felt at peace with our decision. It was not until she finished her last final on the morning of graduation day that she accepted the fact that she would be walking on the stage that evening to receive her diploma.

As we were getting dressed for her graduation ceremony, she came in, turned me toward her, hugged me, and thanked me for always believing in her, being in her corner, allowing her to be who she is, and guiding her in the right direction in life. We paused for a moment to discuss the importance of stress and balance, talking about how stress and anxiety can lead to various health and well-being issues. We both agreed that it equals burnout.

As I reflect on my personal crossroads, I realize that balancing socialization at any age is both a personal evolution and a necessity for emotional well-being. I can say my needs, capacities, and desires for connection are changing. I'm not saying I need to become less social, but I do need to become more selective, intentional, and reflective about where my energy is going. I always thought self-care was being social because it involved fun and positivity. As I emotionally balance myself, I realize that choosing balance is not about doing less; it is about doing what nourishes your spirit. Burnout, anxiety, and stress are not signs of weakness but signals that one's soul is asking for rest. Turning the page means honoring a truthful message of reclaiming peace and stepping into the next chapter with grace. We all deserve a life that feels good on the inside, not just one that looks good on the outside.

I have learned to pray whenever I want, pause and enjoy quiet time, lie in bed longer, turn off my phone, turn off the TV, and say no, all to enjoy peace. As I reflected on my personal crossroads, I realized how and why certain things happened, which caused me to turn the page and focus on my overall self-care. This is about taking proactive steps to manage my well-being across multiple levels of life and protect my energy because I have learned that energy is sacred.

"I am not just surviving—I am ***sovereign***—and this life is mine to live, fully and freely."

Chapter 5:

My Mistakes Don't Define Me

Jessika Allen

Today, I woke up feelin' rich… in my low-income apartment. I know that might sound crazy to some, but to me? That's wealth. Peace is wealth. Progress is wealth. I remember being 17, a brand-new mom, living in Gastonia, North Carolina, trying to get into one of those low-income housing programs. I'd apply for every lottery that came open and would get denied over and over. Felt like the same girls had been living in those spots forever, never moving out. No turnover meant no chance. I was out here with a baby on my hip, sleeping on people's couches, feeling like I was at the bottom of the list.

Then I had my second child at 24, and by then? It was like the world had given me a red stamp: DENIED. Criminal charges. Bad decisions. My name was flagged in every system. Every application was a no. Every letter felt like a reminder of my past. I was labeled. Branded. And yet, something in me never gave up. So, the day I finally got approved for affordable housing? Man, it felt like I made it for real. That little apartment key in my hand might as well have been a key to a mansion in Beverly Hills.

But now I see it. God had a plan all along. Had I gotten into one of those housing spots back at 17, I probably would've stayed stuck, complacent, maybe on welfare, just settling. That mindset I had back then? Survival mode. Trapped in my environment. I didn't know nothin' about elevation, growth, or healing. But now? Whew. I understand how to use my resources as stepping stones. Not crutches. And that's the difference.

I was deep in them streets. That's all I knew. My environment, my people, they were all I had, and they were in survival mode too. I was around people who normalized struggle. Like pain was a badge of honor. I remember my aunt looking me in the face one day and saying, "What? You tryna be on welfare your whole life?" And that stuck with me. Because she was someone I looked up to—still do. She didn't say it to tear me down. She said it to wake me up.

I was born in Oroville, California. That small town holds a lot. I moved to Gastonia, NC when I was 14. That shift was major from a little Cali girl with a wild streak to a Southern teen navigating culture shock and starting over. I was thrown into a whole new world. New accents. New rules. New struggles. I had to adjust quickly. Being the oldest meant wearing a mask. I had to be perfect. Strong. Unshakable. But inside? I was tired. I didn't know how to say it.

We weren't wealthy growing up, but we were rich in spirit. Our family was close-knit. I had both sides—my Mexican heritage and my Black heritage. I call myself "Blaxican"—a lil humor amid the chaos. My mama? A soldier. She worked hard to keep us afloat, including my stepdad. They did what they could with what they had. We didn't always have new things, but we had love and a strong will to survive. When we moved to NC, it was supposed to be a fresh start, but it felt like I was reborn in a storm. I struggled to find my place.

I've always been a helper. That's just who I am. Since I was little, I've carried people. Held my brothers down like they were my own babies. I'm my brother's keeper. Period. And if it wasn't for my mama, I wouldn't be the kind of mother I am today. She did the best she could, even while battling her own demons. Her trauma tried to bleed into me, but she still protected us as much as she could. That overprotection? It shaped me.

Some pain is inevitable. I learned that word from my biological father. He was locked up most of my life, but I remember this one time when he got out. He looked at me and said, "You being born was inevitable." Funny how that word stuck with me. We didn't have a close bond. I asked him once why he never called or checked on me. He told me, "Out of sight, out of mind." And he was talkin' about me. His firstborn. That moment? It changed me. Hardened me. Made me crave something deeper, something real. I looked for love in the wrong places after that.

I was still in high school, still trying to figure out who I was—but now I had a baby dependin' on me. I hustled. Worked after school. Sold candy. Did hair in my kitchen. I was always grinding. Not just for me, but for my homegirls, my people. I've always been that one. The strong friend. The go-getter. But under that strength? I was tired. I was lost. I was angry. I wanted love. I wanted security. I wanted a real man to show up for me and my child.

That's how I ended up in too many toxic relationships. Looking for something in people who didn't even have it for themselves. I tolerated pain. I normalized dysfunction. I thought struggle was love. And all that did was bury me deeper. Into the streets. Into survival. Into moments that still haunt me.

But let me say this loud: I regret none of it. Because without those chapters, I wouldn't be the woman I am now. I wouldn't know resilience. I wouldn't have the testimony. I wouldn't be able to stand in front of a room full of women and say, "Sis, I made it out. You can too."

So when I say I woke up feeling rich in my little apartment? I mean, I woke up feeling favored. Because I know what it's like to be without. To feel invisible. To be judged. To be counted out. I've been at rock bottom more than once. But I never stayed there. I refused.

Now I teach other women how to stand up. I use my story as a blueprint. I build businesses. I mentor. I show up. Because someone out there needs to see that healing is possible, that transformation is real, and that God don't make no mistakes.

From Section 8 to self-made. From felon to founder. From teen mom to empowered mama. From silence to a voice that can't be silenced. That's me. That's my legacy.

And baby, I'm just getting started.

"With Pain, Comes Strength"

Today, I can look in the mirror and see a woman who survived it all. But let me take you back, because there was a time when I didn't even recognize the girl looking back at me. This is the raw, unfiltered truth—the part of my story that I used to be ashamed to tell. Now? It's the part I speak loudest about, because I know another woman out there is fighting to survive, too.

I got into a relationship with a man I didn't even know. Sounds crazy, right? But when you're craving love so bad you'll take it from anyone, even if it's wrapped in red flags, you miss the signs. I had just moved back to California from North Carolina, 21 years old, still just a baby in so many ways. Still healing from wounds I hadn't even named. Still chasing something that felt like home. June 8th, 2012—that's the day we made it to Chico, CA, after living 8 years in North Carolina. I'll never forget it because it was the same birthday as an old flame from my high school days in North Carolina. Ain't it funny how dates follow you? It's like the universe trying to remind you of the cycles you need to break.

The streets introduced me to Superman. He was in prison, locked up, and somehow, I felt more connected to Superman than I had with anyone else. Why? Because I was desperate to feel chosen. That's what the streets teach you when you grow up without a father—you keep searching for that man who will love you unconditionally. I've said it before, and I'll repeat it: "Girls who grow up without their daddies spend their whole lives trying to fill that void." I was that girl. Gabrielle Union once said, "We live in a world where we all need each other, and yet, too many of us are isolated." Whew. That was me—physically surrounded but spiritually alone.

We started off writing letters, late-night phone calls from correctional facilities. It felt deep. It felt loyal. I thought I was being ride-or-die, but baby, I was dying slowly. When he got out, the abuse didn't start with fists. It started with words. "You ain't going nowhere." "No one else gon' want you." "You lucky I even deal with you." His favorite one was, " You know you done fucked up, right," and he would laugh in my face while saying it. That type of mental warfare will eat you alive. I was isolated. He didn't want me hanging with my girls, didn't want me seeing my family. I'd wake up and not even recognize my own life.

And the worst part? I thought it was love. I thought real love required sacrifice. I thought being his peace meant staying quiet while I was breaking inside. Taraji P. Henson once said, "We, as Black women, don't talk about mental health. We just keep pushing. But we are hurting." That quote stuck with me because that was my life. I was pushing through trauma, masking pain with loyalty, and calling it love.

I was doing things I never imagined—some for money, some for survival, some to please him. I let him manipulate my mind so much that I brought girls around, thinking I was proving my loyalty, trying to impress him. He flirted with them, disrespected me, and I smiled through it. I was numb. Emotionally dead inside but still trying to look alive on the outside.

"Jeremiah 29:11"

"For I know the plans I have for you," declares the LORD, "plans to prosper you and not to harm you, plans to give you hope and a future. Then you will call on me and come and pray to me, and I will listen to you. You will seek me and find me when you seek me with all your heart."

I remember the night he said he was going to the gym at 4 a.m.

That's when I felt it. That voice in my spirit whispered, *"He lying."* But I was too drained to argue. You get to a point in a toxic relationship where your body is present, but your spirit is on life support. I didn't have the strength to fight anymore. I just laid there, numb, pretending to sleep while a part of me shattered quietly inside.

The next morning, something told me to check his phone. And there it was—like confirmation from the universe. A text to another woman: *"Are you available?"*

Just three words. But those three words ripped me apart.

That wasn't just cheating. That was betrayal stacked on top of emotional abuse, manipulation, broken promises, and years of sacrifice. I had poured everything into him. My money, my time, my loyalty—even my peace. And that's what I got in return?

We argued. We screamed. We fought from one block to the next. Neighbors came outside, lights turned on, and blinds moved. Somebody called the cops.

And what did I do? I stood right there, heart crushed, spirit shaking, still trying to protect him.

"I'll go," I told the cops. "He ain't from here. I'll stay at my mama's."

Still loyal. Still covering for a man who had done nothing but expose me to pain. But baby—plot twist—they didn't take him. They took me.

Felony domestic violence.

Let me repeat that for the people in the back: *felony. Domestic. Violence.*

Me. A single mother. A woman with no violent history. Facing 5–7 years for a man who should've been facing judgment himself. I was in shock. My hands were cuffed, and I remember looking back thinking, *"How did I become the villain in my own story?"*

The police were just at my apartment days before because he was holding me against my will while I was screaming for my life. He hid in the closet, and I covered for him like a dummy. You would think they had a record of that call and looked into it before throwing me in cuffs.

I remembered something Oprah said: *"Turn your wounds into wisdom."* At that point, all I had were wounds—deep, invisible ones that didn't show up in X-rays but ran through every part of me. But I was about to get a crash course in what wisdom really cost.

Jail.

Stripped down to nothing but an orange jumpsuit. No lashes. No nails. No filters. No phones. No mirrors. Just metal bunks, cold floors, and thoughts that scream louder than any jail siren ever could. I cried myself hoarse the first few nights. My pillow? Thin. My hope? Thinner.

I prayed. I journaled. I wrote letters I never sent.

One morning, in the dayroom, we were watching the local news. And there it was.

My house. On TV. In flames.

While I was locked up, Superman threw a party. A house party. At my place. Where my babies lay their heads, and somehow, it turned into a shootout. Gunfire in my home—*and I wasn't even there.*

I felt rage bubble up in my chest. I was sitting in a cell for *defending myself*, and this man was out here turning my home into a warzone. All I could think was, *"Do y'all see who the real criminal is?"*

But the system didn't care. They never do. They don't look at the evidence. They don't look at the pain. They look at your name, your record, your address—and they check a box.

I had the texts. I had the emails. I had bruises, stories, and tears. None of it mattered.

Taraji once said in an interview, *"Black women suffer in silence—and then get punished when we finally scream."* And that's precisely what happened to me. I screamed. And I was punished.

But even in there, God wasn't done with me.

That's when I found Jeremiah 29:11.

"For I know the plans I have for you..."

I met a woman named Michael. Yeah, Michael. She said straight up, "God sent me here to save you." And maybe she was right. One night, she slid me a piece of paper with scriptures written on it in pencil. One of them hit me like lightning, "Jeremiah 29:11." I stayed up all night reading the entire chapter of Jeremiah.

I folded that paper and hid it as if it were a million-dollar check. That night, I slept for the first time in weeks.

Michael gave me hope. That scripture gave me air. In the most hopeless place, I found a crack of light.

And just when I thought I had already been through enough, betrayal came knocking again—this time from someone even closer.

I called my sister to check in on things.

Trina.

My best friend. She used to sleep at my house. My mama used to buy her Christmas presents. We were *sisters*. She told me she had a business opportunity, and she knew I had a little savings for a cruise I was planning for my son's and my birthday.

"Just loan me $5,000," she said. "I'll pay you back $7,000 when the contract hits."

I wired her the money—from California to North Carolina. We had plans. She was supposed to pick me up from the jail when I was released. Instead? She ghosted me. Didn't answer. No texts. No calls.

I had my cousin ride over to her house.

Empty

No furniture.

No Trina.

Blocked.

Gone.

Have you ever been betrayed by somebody you fed? Housed? Prayed for? That pain hit different. That kind of betrayal slices you open in places even trauma didn't reach. I had put people on, invested in folks, given out love and game like it was free water. And time after time, I got stabbed in the back.

The Breakthrough

When I finally got out of jail, I was different.

Not stronger yet—just harder.

My heart was calloused. My hope was dusty. I didn't walk out a warrior—I walked out *wounded.* I was angry. Angry at the system. At the man. At the so-called friends. At myself.

I had nothing.

No job.

No home.

No car.

No plan.

Just me and my kids—and a lot of rage.

I crashed at my mama's for a while. Slept in garages, closets, even cars some nights. I was homeless—but even more than that, I felt spiritually homeless. Everyone else's life went on while mine had been paused, rewound, and erased.

I walked for miles some days. Caught the bus. Whatever I had to do to maintain. I hated the "you're strong" comments. I hated the fake support. I hated that I had to start from scratch while others were living well off the things I had grinded hard for.

My little brothers—especially Kee—were close to my son. That bond saved me more than they'll ever know. It reminded me I still had purpose, even when everything else felt gone.

Starting over was like learning to breathe again, with lungs full of grief and betrayal.

But here's the thing.

Eventually... I did start breathing again.

I started rising.

Started creating.

Started healing.

I didn't want my story to end in pain. I wanted it to serve as a testimony. I wanted to be living proof that even if you're discarded, you can still rise.

I started pouring into other women. Started sharing my truth. I turned my wounds into wisdom. I took the labels they tried to slap on me—*felon*, *angry*, *statistic*—and turned them into fuel.

Now I'm walking in purpose. Not perfection—purpose.

Jeremiah 29:11 wasn't just a verse I read in jail—it became my life's foundation. *"Plans to prosper you and not to harm you..."* That promise kept me alive. That promise became my reality.

Because God's plans?

They're greater than your pain.

I was placed on probation for a period of three years. It felt like I was walking on eggshells, constantly looking over my shoulder. I had to enroll in a 52-week domestic violence program—strict rules, no leniency. You couldn't be late, couldn't miss more than two classes, and even if you did miss one, you still had to pay. Each class was $45, and the instructors made it worse. They rotated so often, making it hard to build trust or stability, which was already something we were all struggling to find.

Some of us girls are just coming home from jail, trying to re-enter society, still in recovery, still unstable. The system didn't care about the trauma we were carrying. They didn't consider what it meant to force women, fresh out of chaos, into a rigid program with no flexibility or compassion. It felt like they set us up to fail.

There was an instructor named Lauren. She tried to connect by talking about motherhood, but it didn't land well. She spoke in a childish voice as if we were little girls and always had something opinionated to say. It felt more performative than genuine. What we needed was someone who could relate from experience, not sympathy, but understanding.

Showing up to those classes every week in the middle of the day made it nearly impossible to keep a job. But I did what I had to do. I met two girls there who became my closest friends. One of them passed away, and the other fell deep into one of the deepest addictions, she changed from inside out right in front of me. That hurt, watching people I loved fall through the cracks.

Boundaries saved me, not only from others but also from myself—my habits, guilt, and my tendency to fix others before healing myself. As Tyler Perry said through Madea, "No need to build a wall—build a fence so you can see who's coming." I didn't shut everyone out, but I did learn how to protect my peace.

The system isn't set up to support reentry—it's designed to monitor and punish. But through all of it, I kept going. I'm grateful for the few people who rooted for me, even quietly. And I'm proud of myself for becoming the kind of woman who knows when to love others… and when to choose herself first.

Finding Me Again

I got a caregiving job caring for the elderly with memory problems, and it felt like a fresh start. I remember slipping into scrubs, and for a moment, I felt like myself again. It reminded me of my first job at fifteen, working in a medical office with my mom back in North Carolina. Something about putting on those scrubs made me feel proud—like I had a purpose again. I nervously passed the interview, unsure if my big F would show up on the background check after they did my fingerprinting, but I was hired! That joy didn't last long.

About two weeks into the job, I got a letter from the county. It said that, because of my recent violent charge, I could no longer legally work with children or the elderly. My heart dropped. I had a choice—hide it and keep working, or be honest. I decided to tell the supervisor. It took a lot of courage. She was a woman of color, so I thought she might understand. She nodded and said everything would be fine, making it seem like it wasn't a big deal.

The next day, I came in... and they let me go.

That was one of those moments where I really felt the weight of my record. I was trying to do the right thing, trying to be honest—and it backfired. The system said they wanted us to rehabilitate, to reenter society, but at every turn, I felt like I was being punished for trying.

After that, I was placed in a warehouse job—because that's all my record would allow. And even then, I had to schedule everything around my anger management classes every Wednesday at noon, which made it nearly impossible to hold a decent-paying day job. It felt like every door that opened slammed right back in my face.

"Humbled, Then Hired"

Another restriction of probation. Another consequence meant to break me. They called it community service, but let's be real—it felt more like punishment dressed up in a church pamphlet. I was assigned to work at a homeless resource center called Holy Helpers, and from day one, it was degrading. I had to be there by 7:00 a.m. sharp, and if I were even five minutes late, they'd send me home, and I would be facing a violation of my probation requirements. No exceptions. No grace.

Out there in the freezing morning with a trash picker in one hand and a heart full of shame in the other, I picked up used needles, broken bottles, dog shit, cigarette butts, and people's stories off the ground. Manuel, the man who "ran" the place, treated us like we were inmates and he was the warden. Bitter. Bossy. Disrespectful. He had no idea the pain we carried or the fight it took to show up. He didn't care. He and a few of the other fake employees acted like they were God's favorites. But instead of helping the homeless with compassion, they treated everyone like criminals, especially those of us doing community service. It ran like a prison yard.

They had services, yeah. But they picked and chose who got what, and it was sad. They had no genuine trauma-informed care, no love, just judgment. It would break my heart seeing people denied basic things like socks or a blanket just because they mouthed off or were having a mental health episode. Some of the clients were chronically homeless with severe mental illness—I mean, talking to themselves, rocking back and forth, out of touch with reality. Instead of de-escalating or showing empathy, staff would call the cops. My stomach would turn every time. Like, damn, is this how we treat our people?

One sister I met during my hours always wore a long coat, no matter how hot it was outside. She was soft-spoken, delicate, like a bird who'd lost her way. One day, while I was wiping down trays in the kitchen, she came up to me with teary eyes and said, "You remind me of my sister. She died in the streets. You got her spirit." Then she slid a beaded bracelet into my hand. "Keep this. Stay safe."

I took that bracelet and cried the whole way home. I even met one of my current best friends, Chanel, there. She was homeless herself, living in a transitional house, and one time, I broke down. I was at the bottom. Sleeping in my car. We were texting each other, and I told her my situation. The next thing I hear is the sound of money that the Cash App makes on your phone, "ching, ching, ching!" This girl sent me $200!!! I barely knew her then. We are friends to this day, our daughters have grown up close to each other, and even have matching tattoos.

They thought that place would break me, but it awakened something within me instead. It humbled me. And in that humility, I found purpose.

I cleaned filthy toilets, scrubbed showers, and did laundry full of strangers' socks and underwear. I handed out food trays while getting called names—"bitch," "n*****," "slut." I kept my head down, prayed under my breath, and kept moving. And through all that, I realized something deeper: I actually liked helping people. I didn't need a paycheck to feel valuable. I needed to know I made someone feel seen.

Even while I was broke, serving time on the outside, I was being built. The cook became my friend—he was this older Black man with a raspy voice and a wild past. He told me about his time on the streets, his journey through addiction, and how one day he just decided to start over.

There was also an older couple who came in for Bible study. They remembered me from jail. "Ain't no coincidence God put us back in your path," the wife said once. They used to smuggle in little scriptures or messages for me when they visited my brother. I often sat with them, eating the center's food because I had nothing at home. I mean *nothing.* I'd wrap leftovers up in napkins to take something home to feed myself, and sometimes my babies, too. That's how real it was.

One day, during my walk around the block with that raggedy-ass trash picker, I saw a house. Big. Grey. "For Rent" sign swinging like a miracle in the wind. Something in me said, *Call.* I don't know what came over me. I wasn't supposed to believe in myself. I was a felon. I was in community service. I was broke.

But I called.

And I got it.

Me.

That house was right around the corner from the center. It had a big yard, a wide porch, hardwood floors that creaked with pride. I moved in with my little brother. That same house is where he and his now wife brought their first baby home. That house became a milestone I never expected to see coming.

I started healing, not just surviving—healing. I poured into myself in ways I never had before. I journaled. I started listening to Michelle Obama's podcasts, TED Talks, and motivational speeches. I had Sarah Jakes Roberts on repeat, listening to every message and interview. I took my first hike to Monkey Face with a boy named Bear, whom I liked. That hike was a spiritual moment—it was a declaration: I'm coming back to myself. I'm climbing out. I began connecting to nature like never before, and I started practicing meditation and sound healing. This was all so new to me, and I felt a deep connection. I started being okay with being in my own presence. Yes! Co-dependency is real, and I had struggled with that along with abandonment issues for a very long time.

The Shift

A relative who worked at a shelter told me they were hiring. I almost laughed. *Me? Work at a shelter?* After what I just went through? Flashbacks of Manuel, that toxic-ass place, being barked at like a dog…

But something whispered: *Try.*

I applied. I interviewed. And I got the job.

Now, I was in the position Manuel had. But I wasn't about to be another Manuel.

I showed up every day ready to change the culture. I brought snacks. I brought patience. I brought grace. I asked people how they were doing, really. I remembered their names. I didn't treat mental illness like a threat—I treated it like pain that needed love.

Maya Angelou once said, *"People will forget what you said, people will forget what you did, but people will never forget how you made them feel."* I wanted every person that walked through our doors to feel like they mattered—even if they hadn't showered in a month, even if they were yelling at shadows, even if they were still battling their demons.

I became a case manager. I started running groups. I became the woman I needed when I was lost.

Community service didn't break me. It saved me. It showed me the truth of the system and planted a seed of purpose. It taught me how broken things can still be beautiful. And how some of us are sent to shine light in the darkest corners of the world.

As Tupac once said, *"I might not change the world, but I guarantee I will spark the brain that will."* And baby, my brain got sparked picking up trash in an alley.

You never know what chapter God is writing while you think you're still stuck in the intro.

Humbled, then hired.

That's how it started.

But trust me... it gets deeper.

"Built From Betrayal"

I had many adversities in my work environment when I started off, but this right here? This was another lesson meant to make me stronger. If I had known back then where these struggles would lead me, I would've just rode the wave with my head high instead of stressing. But we don't know that when we're in the thick of it. Our traumas don't come with labels or a cheat code like a board game showing us the next move. We just learn as we go, and that's what I did—every painful step at a time.

Community service hours led me to a shelter job in January 2019. What started as a court-ordered task became the beginning of my career. I got hired as a Lead Monitor, and not long after, I was doing case management. Me—a felon—creating case plans, advocating for DV survivors, helping women get into housing. I wasn't supposed to be the one helping, not by society's standards. But I was. I became what I once needed. The struggle became my foundation.

I saw myself in every woman I helped. Every intake form felt personal. I knew what it was like to sleep in cars, to survive off nothing, to feel invisible. So I spoke up, loud. I learned the housing system like the back of my hand, found the legal loopholes, and used them to speak life into women who were broken down just like I used to be.

But that glow? Not everyone liked it. If you've ever read *The 48 Laws of Power*, you know rule #1—never outshine the master. But baby, I was shining without even trying. My light intimidated people. I became a target for workplace hostility. My passion, my advocacy—it started to ruffle feathers. I wasn't trying to be a threat. I was just doing the work. But even that was too much for some.

One of the people I looked up to was this man named James. He had also been formerly incarcerated, and I thought we could relate. I even asked him to help with my Letter of Interest when I applied for the case management position. It took him 'til the night before to give me any feedback, and what he sent felt more like something to tear me down than build me up. He used big words to intimidate me, like I wasn't smart enough.

Later, I realized this same man—this person I thought was a brother—had followed me through the years, sabotaging me. I remember him cutting up my pictures in the breakroom like we were kids. He would compete with me over clients, undermining their needs just to "win." Residents would come to me, saying he was being inappropriate—touching, stalking, crossing lines. Then he turned that same creepy energy on me. I had trusted him, but he became a stalker, a sick man hiding behind a professional title.

I gave my heart to that job. I joined a committee, volunteered endless hours trying to build something real for the staff, for the people. But it was all fake. The promises, the meetings, the "we're in this together"—all lies. I got burned. That's when I realized: I can't keep hiding in someone else's shadow, feeding someone else's dreams. I had to put myself first.

I left that job too and I accepted a job offer from a friend who was building her own nonprofit. I admired her vision—it looked good on social media, and I wanted to be a part of it. I didn't apply through no website. I hit her directly, thinking, "Let me support a Black woman doing her thing." She offered me the Assistant Director position. Solid pay. Good title. I was hyped.

But from the jump, it was giving disorganized. No onboarding, no structure—just Zoom calls talking about million-dollar grants and ideas. I was putting in serious work. Still working my 9–5, going to school part-time, doing hair, raising two kids. I juggled it all because I believed in her mission. I gave that role my time, my mind, my passion.

For four whole months, I was doing the most—without a check to show for it. Finally, I asked for mileage reimbursement, just to cover gas for all the running around I was doing. That's when everything shifted. Her energy changed. Suddenly, I was "too busy," and she demoted me through a text message. Not a phone call. Not a meeting. A damn text.

That shit broke me. Real tears. I had skipped assignments and ended up getting kicked out of college, reduced hours at my actual paying job, put my own business on hold—just to support what I thought was a powerful legacy project. I believed in her. And she turned around and played me.

The kicker? At our last meeting, she brought in this white girl. No experience. No credentials. And started onboarding her in front of me using documents I had created. I was floored. She smiled at me afterward and said, "We need to talk about finally getting you onboarded."

Six months later? Girl, please.

I sat there, swallowing my pride, trying to hold it together. After the meeting, she looked me dead in the face and said, "So what are you even capable of?" Then said I was a liability to her organization.

I had prayed in the car before that meeting, asking God to keep my spirit calm. I just wanted to be wrong. But nah—He revealed the truth. She opened the conversation with, "I'm a real bitch…" and at that point, I knew the professionalism had left the chat. I stood up and said, "Yeah, this ain't gonna work." And walked out with my head held high.

I drove straight to Martin Luther King Park—my childhood park—and cried. That deep cry. Not a "why me," but a "why are people like this?" My mom pulled up slapping S.O.S Band " No One's Gonna Love You." She has always done the littlest things to make me happy, She has always showed up and made something outta nothing even when she had absolutely nothing. She knew something was off. I'd told her everything from day one, and she had been praying it would work out. But mamas always know.

As I sat there, broken, she said something that stuck: "If she deactivates your work email, you won't have access to that training you've been working so hard on." I didn't want to believe it. This woman had missed every other deadline—surely she wouldn't move that fast.

But by the time I got home, the email was gone. She moved quick when it came to taking something from me. I lost access to all the training hours and my certification process. I was crushed.

That night, I laid in bed in a fog. Couldn't sleep. Couldn't think. Just stuck in that place of "How do people get away with this?"

I call them culture vultures. They drive Teslas, wear designer, and brag about grant money while never stepping foot in the communities they claim to serve. They don't serve plates, don't lift voices. They exploit pain for profit. They're in it for the image, not the impact.

But my mama's words echoed in my head: "They gon' need you before you need them."

And she was right.

It took me a minute to bounce back. I was in a funk, questioning myself, doubting my worth. But then that fighter in me woke back up. I wasn't about to let anyone steal my joy or my future. I reached out to the training company, explained everything. Because the account was in my name, they reset the email. I got my access back.

That same night, I stayed up until 1 a.m. and finished that certification.

That paper wasn't just a certificate—it was proof. Proof that I can't be broken. That even when people try to play you, block you, underestimate you, you can still win.

This is the type of shit people don't talk about. The behind-the-scenes grind. The heartbreak in nonprofit spaces. The way people in your own community will step on you to get ahead.

But guess what? I'm still here.

And I'm still building.

Because my mission ain't for the likes, or the check, or the clout. It's for the people. It's for that girl crying in her car after being let down again. It's for the mamas trying to juggle everything and still make it work. It's for the folks who've been counted out, overlooked, and silenced.

I do it for us.

And I'm never letting go of my power again.

Jeremiah 29:11-14

"For I know the plans"

Full circle. That's the only way I can explain it. Life has a way of spinning the block, and if you hold on long enough—if you stay down, loyal to your soil, if you trust God through the grime and the grief—you'll rise. You'll glow. You'll sit in the same rooms you used to mop the floors in.

And *baby*, that's exactly what happened to me.

I used to pick up dog shit and needles for community service at a homeless shelter—under a man named Manuel, who barked orders at me like I wasn't even human. Now? I ended up as his Supervisor. Yeah… *his* boss. Talk about a plot twist.

I used to be a client, sitting on the other side of the desk, trying to find housing for my kids. I was at the bottom—dirty, broke, angry. But now? I'm the Assistant Executive Director at a nonprofit. I stepped up and became the Interim Executive Director, leading the same kind of programs that once helped me survive. I'm the one setting the tone. Making decisions. Hiring staff. Changing systems.

"Remember Lauren—the woman who used to be my instructor in that anger management class? I saw her again recently, only this time I was the one in the leadership role. Now she collaborates with me, not out of support, but because she has no choice. Still no compassion, still talking childish—but that's okay. It feels good to let my success speak for itself. I don't need to prove anything. Just showing up as who I am now is more than enough."

And Superman? The same man who once dragged me through hell. The one who hurt me in ways I couldn't even explain at the time. I saw him on the news last year—in some serious trouble facing some life-altering charges.

I didn't celebrate. I didn't smile. But I did recognize that life always gives back what it owes and pain has a way of circling back.

I'm a business owner now. I just signed the lease on my own office space—GMG Styles: The Legacy Lounge, my own damn office space. I set my own hours, choose my own clients, and run my own show. I pulled off the lot in a 2025, brand-new car, with my name on the papers. Nobody can take that from me. I fought for it. I bled for it. And I *prayed* for it.

"All things are possible through Christ who strengthens me."

—Philippians 4:13

And baby, let me tell you—if I knew then what I know now?! Believe half of what you see and none of what you hear. Whew. Growth is a hell of a thing.

I visited that same aunt this year. I even took my kids on a cruise to Mexico. We stay vacationing. First time back in North Carolina in like eight years. It was a whole healing trip. I took my kids with me and made it a real vacation. My daughter? Lit up packin' her suitcase like it was the Grammys. My son? Proud as hell that I followed through and took him to see his daddy—to show him where he came from, his roots.

She was the one making sure we had everything ready. She kept calling before we left, trying to plan all the trip details. I couldn't tell if she was stressed or just being her usual, over-the-top loving self. She had food, rides, space—everything waiting for us.

But *this* time, I was ready. I felt like a real grown woman when we landed. I booked us a rental car all by myself—even after the chaos the night before. Because let me tell you, it was a mess…

We missed our flight and ended up in a trap motel in South Natomas, Sacramento. I was stressed out and mad at myself. I had even left my bank card at home—rookie mistake. And you know how those rental places are: no debit cards, no Apple Pay, no Cash App. Name-on-the-card or nothing. I felt defeated.

But God had me. I had my little TikTok "100 Envelope Savings Challenge" book with me. Random, right? But guess what—it had all my paid-off credit cards inside. Maybe it was trauma, perhaps it was divine planning—but either way, I was covered.

We stayed in a brand-new hotel for a week. Clean. Comfortable. Safe. I took care of everything—myself and my kids. I was able to move with grace, ease, and confidence. That's growth.

I woke up every morning grateful. My kids were laughing and well-fed, and now this book opportunity? C'mon now. That's *favor.*

"I am the rose that grew from concrete."

—Tupac Shakur

I was the one folks whispered about, the one they counted out. But God never gave up on me.

And now? I'm out here sitting in council meetings, in boardrooms, at national conferences, speaking up for my people, for the system-involved, the overlooked, the forgotten. From the trap to the table, baby. And I walk in like I *belong*—because I do.

I got my record expunged. My name is clean. My spirit is even cleaner. I'm back in school, not because I have to, but because I want to. I want more. I am more.

I'm a mother, a healer, a stylist, and now an author. Yeah, sis! And don't let anybody tell you that you aren't CAPABLE because YOU ARE!. I'm telling my story. And I'm not ashamed, nor am I done. Because now I know: my story is my *superpower.*

"Healing doesn't mean the damage never existed. It means the damage no longer controls you."

—Iyanla Vanzant

Some people only remember the version of you that you used to be. Let them. God saw the healed version. The bossed-up version. The abundant version.

Not everything is for you. Some doors stay closed because what's behind them would've destroyed you. Let them stay shut.

Protect your peace. Be selective. Not everyone deserves access to the new you.

"Sis, stop explaining yourself to people committed to misunderstanding you."

—Megan Thee Stallion

Growth ain't cute. It's messy. Lonely. Exhausting. But it's worth it.

This is what *Living in Her Abundance on Purpose* looks like:

- Being in rooms I once cleaned.
- Hiring people who once doubted me.
- Starting businesses I dreamed of in jail.
- Driving cars I thought I'd never qualify for.
- Taking trips I used to beg God for.
- Writing chapters I once thought nobody would read.

So, if you're reading this? And you're still in the *dark part* of your story? *Don't give up.*

Your full circle is coming. Keep pushing. Keep praying. Keep building. God's not done with you yet.

You are not your mistakes. You are not your past. You are a concrete rose—rooted in power, grown in pain, and glowing in purpose.

Jessika Allen~ gmgstyles@outlook.com

Chapter 6:

A Champion's Journey

Mayra Colon

Introduction

It is with great pleasure and a humble heart that I welcome you into this chapter, which I have titled *A Champion's Journey*. My name is Mayra. I'm originally from Puerto Rico, and English is my second language. I share this to offer perspective on my cultural background and how I relate and write my story. I'm a daughter, a mother, a grandmother, and a friend. I'm a believer and follower of the Messiah. I work in the healthcare field and consider myself a blessed woman.

I am the author of the book *"I Am a Champion," written for people like you and me who don't always win,* but never stop fighting. That's the essence of a true champion. We often admire famous athletes and artists, focusing solely on their success. Rarely do we consider the daily struggles and the journey that led them there. One thing all champions share is this: they never give up. That's what I want to share with you in this chapter.

Background

We all come from unique backgrounds and circumstances that shape who we are and how we perceive life. Parents usually try their best to raise their children, but many external factors influence our learned behaviors and worldview.

I was raised in a strict, controlling, fear-based household. Religion was the central pillar, coupled with a constant concern for "what others might think or say." Intentional wrongdoing and honest mistakes were treated the same. This rigid religiosity and cultural pressure stifled my growth and delayed my development. I lived in fear and constant self-doubt.

Our family lived with a mindset of scarcity. While our finances were limited, the deeper issue was the belief that change was impossible. There was no encouragement to dream bigger or aim higher. This mentality extended beyond finances to emotional, physical, and spiritual realms. I grew up seeking approval, never feeling good enough, and constantly trying to please others—losing myself in the process. I felt shame, guilt, fear, loneliness, and dissatisfaction, regardless of how hard I tried or what I achieved.

At school, I avoided conflict because I didn't know how to stand up for myself. I bottled up emotions, resulting in extreme emotional responses—either overly passive or passive-aggressive. I cried when I couldn't express myself or lashed out with words when overwhelmed, indifferent to the consequences. I wanted to be outgoing and successful but had no idea how to achieve that. I often submitted to those who mistreated me and pushed away those who were kind. This dysfunction made it difficult to build close, healthy relationships. I made friends easily but often adapted myself to please others, hoping someone would eventually love me for who I was.

I wasn't athletic, artistic, or popular. I was simply trying to survive. Despite having good grades and a sharp mind, I constantly searched for belonging and never felt like I fit in. Religion, poverty, and lack of support caused me to repeat harmful choices.

I believed that to be biblically and socially accepted, I had to achieve a perfect blend of ethics, morality, education, health, and financial stability. These were noble aspirations, but the expectations were unrealistic—perfection was the goal, and perfection is impossible. Despite my academic achievements and fulfilling life roles, I still felt incomplete.

I longed for someone to complete me and give me value. Like the song says, I was "looking for love in all the wrong places." I attracted people who dropped out of school, used drugs or alcohol, and relied on me entirely while giving little in return. I provided not just emotional support but also shelter, food, transportation, and money—all in exchange for love. But over time, I felt more and more empty. Each failed relationship led to another just like it.

These patterns drained me. I lost more of myself with each repetition. I became numb and disconnected from joy. Even when something was good or beautiful, I felt only regret and sorrow. No one could change my mind; I found the negative in everything and spiraled into self-pity. I believed happiness was reserved for others—not me.

I couldn't tell real love or friendship from false ones. I attracted people who walked the opposite path from mine. I accepted any attention, thinking others would eventually recognize my worth and change. I formed bad habits and entered toxic relationships just to feel seen. I experimented with drugs and alcohol, which worsened my emotional instability. My judgment declined, and I grew more reckless. I kept giving and giving, hoping for love in return, but rarely received it.

In these relationships, I endured emotional, physical, sexual, spiritual, and financial abuse. Dysfunction became my norm. My childhood had left me unprepared, and my adult life chipped away at what little strength I had left.

Eventually, I began to break. The emotional weight I had carried for years started affecting my physical health and spirit. My relationships became strained. I felt alone—even in a crowd. Loneliness wrapped around me like a heavy blanket. I could no longer pretend.

I hated my life. I was uncomfortable in my own skin. Though I never acted on them, I silently wished it would end. The more I searched for answers, the more lost I felt. I didn't know how to name my pain. I could describe the symptoms, but I didn't understand the cause.

All I knew was that I was sick. Life felt meaningless. I was sad, anxious, and constantly exhausted. I was consumed by people-pleasing and obsessed with others' opinions. Why did I keep repeating these destructive cycles? Why couldn't I let go of harmful relationships? I knew I deserved better, but the unhealthy felt familiar. Letting go felt like a loss, not a solution. The emotional wounds were deep, and the pain overwhelming. I needed healing—but didn't know how to begin.

Turning Point

Eventually, I sought therapy again. This time, my therapist recommended codependency podcasts and videos. We began working through the 12-step recovery model. The more I listened, the more I saw my life reflected in the stories. I realized I had been suffering from codependency.

As defined in the *International Journal of Mental Health and Addiction*, codependency means devoting all your emotional and mental energy to someone else at the expense of your own wellbeing.

As a healthcare professional with a degree in human behavior, I had heard of codependency, but I never imagined it applied to me. I thought I was simply being kind and selfless. In truth, I had been sacrificing myself for others' happiness.

Once I understood the root of my illness, I became determined to heal. I reflected on my life like a film, tracing patterns back to childhood. Through therapy, journaling, and reading, I began to break free from fear, doubt, and guilt. I learned that I needed to love and value myself more than anyone else. The purpose I had been searching for had always been within me.

Shift I realized that if I didn't value myself, no one else truly would. If I didn't change, I risked losing my sanity or living a life without joy. I began to see how fortunate I truly was—not an addict, not in prison, not suffering from a chronic illness.

I took stock of my blessings: wonderful children, beautiful grandchildren, a meaningful career, and the enduring love of Abba—my source of unconditional love. He had never abandoned me. I decided my story would be one of a champion—not a victim.

Living the Abundant Life

Today, I live with abundance and purpose. I see my children thriving. My five grandchildren bring joy and pride. My career is stable, and I have the resources to enjoy life. I have meaningful friendships and embrace new adventures. I worship with my faith family and live with joyful anticipation of our Messiah's return.

I've learned that abundance isn't measured in material wealth but in peace of mind, joy, and authentic connection. It's looking in the mirror and knowing you're living true to your values. It's waking up with gratitude and going to sleep without regret.

Encouragement

Yes, life still has challenges. But as Yeshua said, "In this world you will have trouble. But take heart! I have overcome the world." We must seek healing and strength daily. God reminds us: "Be strong and courageous. Do not be afraid or discouraged, for I am with you."

Acknowledge your accomplishments—you've already come further than you think. Healing is possible with faith and action. Awareness is only half the journey; the other half is responsibility and change. We can't live in the past or wait for the future. All we have is today. Use it wisely.

Break the chains of codependency by changing your habits, one step at a time. Don't settle for less. Forgive yourself for your past, knowing that some regrets will remain—but let them remind you how far you've come. See them not as mistakes, but as wisdom earned.

Life will bring distractions—people, problems, and pain. But don't lose sight of your purpose. Make wise choices. Allow grace into your life and have the courage to change direction when needed. You are a champion. Champions don't quit. Even when you rest, you rise again—stronger. You can do all things through Yeshua who strengthens you.

Life's hardships are part of the process. Let them shape you, not break you. Don't rush. Progress steadily, and you'll arrive where you're meant to be. Find safe, supportive people and resources. Take it one day at a time.

How do you know you're healing? You'll know when you choose, every day, to love and care for yourself—not out of selfishness, but because loving yourself allows you to love others better. Wholeness is essential for fulfilling God's purpose for your life. You can support others, but not at the expense of your own wellbeing. This journey out of codependency is lifelong, but I face it with courage and endurance, knowing that my life depends on it.

If my story resonates with you, know this: you're not alone. Every step toward healing reveals your champion's spirit. Keep going. Keep growing.

May the Lord continue to bless you on your own champion's journey.

With love and faith,

Mayra (My-rah)

La Jornada de un Campeón

Por Mayra Colón (Todos los derechos reservados)

Introducción

Es con gran placer y un corazón humilde que te doy la bienvenida a este capítulo, que he titulado *La Jornada de un Campeón*. Mi nombre es Mayra, una mujer hispana-latina nacida en Puerto Rico y criada en Nueva York. Soy una mezcla multicultural que me ha permitido comprender diferentes perspectivas de la vida, lo cual influyen en cómo escribo mi historia. Soy hija, madre, abuela y amiga. Soy creyente y seguidora del Mesías. Trabajo en el campo de la salud y me considero una mujer bendecida.

Soy la autora del libro *Soy una Campeona*, escrito para personas como tú y yo que no siempre ganamos, pero nunca dejamos de luchar. Eso es la esencia de un verdadero campeón. A menudo admiramos a atletas o artistas famosos y nos enfocamos únicamente en su éxito. Rara vez consideramos las luchas diarias y el viaje que los llevó hasta allí. Lo que todos los campeones tienen en común es esto: nunca se rinden. Eso es lo que quiero compartir contigo en este capítulo.

Trasfondo

Todos venimos de entornos y circunstancias únicos que moldean quiénes somos y cómo percibimos la vida. Los padres generalmente hacen lo posible por criar bien a sus hijos, pero hay muchos factores externos que influyen en nuestros comportamientos aprendidos y en nuestra visión del mundo.

Me crié en un hogar estricto, controlador y basado en el miedo. La religión era el pilar central, junto con una preocupación constante por "lo que otros puedan pensar o decir". Se trataba igual a la mala intención y a los errores inocentes. Esta religiosidad rígida y la presión cultural detuvieron mi crecimiento y retrasaron mi desarrollo. Vivía con miedo y duda constante.

Nuestra familia vivía con una mentalidad de escasez. Aunque nuestros recursos financieros eran limitados, el problema más profundo era la creencia de que el cambio era imposible. No había ánimo para soñar en grande o aspirar a más. Esta mentalidad se extendía más allá de lo económico a niveles emocionales, físicos y espirituales. Crecí buscando aprobación, sin sentirme jamás suficiente, y tratando de complacer a los demás, perdiéndome en el proceso. Sentía vergüenza, culpa, miedo, soledad e insatisfacción, sin importar cuánto me esforzara o lo que lograra.

En la escuela evitaba los conflictos porque no sabía cómo defenderme. Reprimía mis emociones, lo que provocaba respuestas extremas—o demasiado pasiva o pasivo-agresiva. Lloraba cuando no podía expresarme o soltaba palabras hirientes cuando estaba abrumada, sin importarme las consecuencias. Quería ser extrovertida y exitosa, pero no tenía idea de cómo lograrlo. A menudo me sometía a quienes me maltrataban y alejaba a quienes eran amables. Esta disfunción dificultó que formara relaciones cercanas y saludables. Hacía amigos con facilidad, pero me adaptaba para complacer a los demás, esperando que alguien me amara por quien era.

No era atlética, ni artística, ni popular. Simplemente trataba de sobrevivir en cada etapa de mi vida. A pesar de tener buenas calificaciones y una mente aguda, buscaba constantemente un sentido de pertenencia y nunca sentí que encajara. La religión, la pobreza y la falta de apoyo me llevaron a repetir decisiones dañinas.

Creía que para ser aceptada bíblica y socialmente, debía lograr una combinación perfecta de ética, moral, educación, salud y estabilidad financiera. Eran aspiraciones nobles, pero las expectativas eran irreales: la perfección era la meta, y la perfección es imposible. A pesar de mis logros académicos y de cumplir mis roles en la vida, seguía sintiéndome incompleta.

Anhelaba que alguien me completara y me diera valor. Como dice la canción, estaba "buscando amor en los lugares equivocados". Atraía a personas que abandonaban la escuela, usaban drogas o alcohol y dependían completamente de mí mientras daban poco a cambio. Proporcionaba no solo apoyo emocional, sino también un techo, comida, transporte y dinero—todo a cambio de amor. Pero con el tiempo, me sentía cada vez más vacía. Cada relación fallida me llevaba a otra igual.

Estos patrones me agotaron. Perdía más de mí misma con cada repetición. Me volví insensible y desconectada de la alegría. Incluso cuando algo era bueno o hermoso, solo sentía remordimiento y tristeza. Nadie podía convencerme de lo contrario; encontraba lo negativo en todo y me sumergía en la autocompasión. Creía que la felicidad era para otros, pero no para mí.

No podía distinguir el amor o la amistad genuinos de los falsos. Atraía a personas que caminaban en la dirección opuesta a la mía. Aceptaba cualquier atención, pensando que otros eventualmente reconocerían mi valor y cambiarían. Adquirí malos hábitos y entré en relaciones tóxicas solo para sentirme vista. Experimenté con drogas y alcohol, lo que empeoró mi inestabilidad emocional. Mi juicio se deterioró y me volví más imprudente. Continué dando y dando, esperando amor a cambio, pero rara vez lo recibía.

En estas relaciones, sufrí abuso emocional, físico, sexual, espiritual y financiero. La disfunción se convirtió en mi norma. Mi infancia no me había preparado, y mi vida adulta agotó la poca fortaleza que tenía.

Eventualmente, comencé a quebrarme. El peso emocional que llevaba durante años empezó a afectar mi salud física y mi espíritu. Mis relaciones se tensaron. Me sentí sola—aunque estuviera rodeada de gente. La soledad me envolvía como una manta pesada. Ya no podía fingir.

Odiaba mi vida. Me sentía incómoda en mi propia piel. Aunque nunca actué, deseaba en silencio que todo terminara. Cuanto más buscaba respuestas, más perdida me sentía. No sabía cómo nombrar mi dolor. Podía describir los síntomas, pero no entendía la causa.

Solo sabía que estaba enferma. La vida carecía de sentido. Estaba triste, ansiosa y constantemente agotada. Me consumía complacer a los demás y obsesionarme con sus opiniones. ¿Por qué repetía estos ciclos destructivos? ¿Por qué no podía alejarme de relaciones dañinas? Sabía que merecía algo mejor, pero lo insalubre se sentía familiar. Dejarlo era como una pérdida, no una solución. Las heridas emocionales eran profundas y el dolor abrumador. Necesitaba sanidad—pero no sabía cómo empezar.

Momento Crucial

Finalmente, busqué terapia nuevamente. Esta vez, mi terapeuta recomendó podcasts y videos sobre codependencia. Comenzamos a trabajar con el modelo de recuperación de 12 pasos. Cuanto más escuchaba, más veía mi vida reflejada en esas historias. Descubrí que había estado sufriendo codependencia.

Según el *International Journal of Mental Health and Addiction*, la codependencia significa dedicar toda tu energía emocional y mental a otra persona a expensas de tu propio bienestar.

Como profesional de la salud con un título en comportamiento humano, había oído hablar de la codependencia, pero nunca imaginé que se aplicara a mí. Pensaba que solo era amable y desinteresada. En realidad, me había sacrificado por la felicidad de los demás.

Una vez que comprendí la raíz de mi enfermedad, decidí sanar. Reflexioné sobre mi vida como una película, rastreando patrones desde mi infancia. A través de la terapia, la escritura y la lectura, comencé a liberarme del miedo, la duda y la culpa. Aprendí que necesitaba amarme y valorarme más que a nadie. El propósito que buscaba siempre estuvo dentro de mí.

Cambio (Shift)

Me di cuenta de que si no me valoraba, nadie más lo haría. Si no cambiaba, corría el riesgo de perder la cordura o vivir sin alegría. Empecé a ver cuán afortunada era de no ser adicta, ni estar en prisión, ni padecer una enfermedad crónica.

Tomé nota de mis bendiciones: hijos maravillosos, nietos hermosos, una carrera significativa y el amor incondicional de Abba—mi fuente de amor. Él nunca me abandonó. Decidí que mi historia sería la de una campeona, no la de una víctima.

Viviendo la Vida Abundante

Hoy vivo con abundancia y propósito. Veo a mis hijos prosperar. Mis cinco nietos me llenan de alegría y orgullo. Mi carrera es estable y tengo los recursos para disfrutar la vida. Tengo amistades significativas y abrazo nuevas aventuras. Adoro con mi familia de fe y vivo con la alegre anticipación del regreso de nuestro Mesías.

He aprendido que la abundancia no se mide por la riqueza material, sino por la paz mental, la alegría y la conexión auténtica. Es mirarte al espejo y saber que vives fiel a tus valores. Es despertar con gratitud y dormir sin remordimientos.

Estímulo

Sí, la vida aún presenta desafíos. Pero como dijo Yeshúa, "En este mundo tendrán aflicciones. Pero ¡animo! Yo he vencido al mundo." Debemos buscar sanidad y fortaleza a diario. Dios nos recuerda: "Sé fuerte y valiente. No temas ni te desalientes, porque yo estoy contigo."

Reconoce tus logros: ya has recorrido más camino del que crees. La sanidad es posible con fe y acción. Ser consciente es solo la mitad del viaje; la otra mitad es tomar acción y tener la valentía de hacer un cambio. No podemos vivir en el pasado ni esperar el futuro. Solo tenemos hoy. Úsalo sabiamente.

Rompe las cadenas de la codependencia cambiando tus hábitos paso a paso. No te conformes con menos. Perdónate por tu pasado, sabiendo que algunos arrepentimientos permanecerán, pero que son recordatorios de cuánto has avanzado. Véelos no como errores, sino como sabiduría ganada.

La vida traerá distracciones: personas, problemas y dolor. Pero no pierdas de vista tu propósito. Toma decisiones sabias. Permite que la gracia entre en tu vida y ten el valor de cambiar de rumbo cuando sea necesario. Eres un campeón. Los campeones no se rinden. Incluso cuando tengas que descansar, vuelve a levantarte—más fuerte. Puedes hacer todas las cosas a través de Yeshúa que te fortalece.

Las dificultades de la vida son parte del proceso. Permíteles moldearte, no destruirte. No te apresures. Avanza con constancia y llegarás donde debes estar. Encuentra personas y recursos seguros y de apoyo. Tómatelo un día a la vez.

¿Cómo sabes que te estás sanando? Lo sabrás cuando elijas, cada día, amarte y cuidarte a ti mismo, no por egoísmo, sino porque amarte te permite amar mejor a los demás. La plenitud es esencial para cumplir el propósito de Dios en tu vida. Puedes apoyar a otros, pero no a costa de tu propio bienestar. Este viaje fuera de la codependencia es de por vida, pero lo afronto con coraje y resistencia, sabiendo que mi vida depende de ello.

Si mi historia resuena contigo, esto debes saber: no estás solo. Cada paso hacia la sanidad revela tu espíritu de campeón. Sigue adelante. Sigue creciendo.

Que el Señor continúe bendiciéndote en tu propio viaje de campeón.

Con amor y fe,

Mayra

Chapter 7:

SHE CAME BACK DIFFERENT: *THE STORY OF A WOMAN WHO CHOSE OBEDIENCE OVER SURVIVAL*

Breauna Chante`

1. A Thousand Lives Behind My Eyes

You ever look at someone and just know—she been through some things? That was me. I didn't have to say a word. My presence did the talking. Pretty, but heavy. Sharp, but tired. I moved like somebody who'd seen too much too soon. And the truth is—I had.

Nobody taught me how to be a woman. I wasn't handed a blueprint on motherhood, healing, or how to lead a family while still bleeding from childhood wounds. What I did have was grit. Hustle. Survival instincts that could put a Navy SEAL to shame. But survival ain't the same as living.

The streets raised me. Circumstances shaped me. I learned early that vulnerability was dangerous. So I built walls. Got sharper. Colder. Quieter.

And that's how I ended up in Philly. Not because it was where I belonged, but because I kept running from the version of me God was trying to call home.

2. The Man Who Looked Like Power

He was older. Rich. White. The kind of man who had everything but peace. He didn't ask for sex. He just wanted my time. My voice. My presence. At first, it felt like a clean hustle. I could talk. I could pretend. I could get paid and dip.

But the deeper I got, the more I realized—this wasn't about money.

He was broken. Obsessive. Dangerous.

Every visit dragged longer. The flattery turned to fixation. One night, he pulled out a shotgun and aimed it straight at my chest. And in that moment, I didn't flinch. I'd already died too many times inside to be scared of dying again.

But something holy rose up in me.

I talked him down. Soft, slow, calculated. I became the calm in his storm. And when he finally crumbled, I found the crack pipe in the bathroom.

That explained everything.

But did I leave?

No.

Because trauma will tell you to stay in rooms that God's been trying to drag you out of.

I told myself I was the one who was in control. That I could stop anytime. That I'd never let it go too far. But the truth is- when someone's paying you thousands just to breathe next to them, it's easy to justify almost anything.

3. Blood Money and Casino Floors

Atlantic City. Presidential suite. Dress on the bed. Five stacks in cash just sitting there like bait. He said he wanted to show me off. Gamble. Laugh. Be his little dream girl for the weekend.

But the air was thick. My spirit was loud. And when he accused me of stealing money he had already gifted me, I knew what it really was—control.

Later, he said he wanted to take me to a jewelry store. Said he was going to buy me an engagement ring. I reminded him this wasn't a real relationship. Told him kindly I couldn't be what he wanted.

And that's when he snapped.

The same rage. The same red face. The same shaking voice. He screamed that Is owed him. That he gave me everything. That I belonged to him.

I ran into the bedroom section of the suite and locked the French doors. Texted my folks the hotel name and the room number.

"If anything happens to me, this is where I am. This is who did it."

After about 45 minutes, he switched up again. He was back to being what he thought was my knight in shining armor.

He knocked gently. Whispered mr nickname like a lullaby.

"Baby cakes… come out. I have a surprise for you."

I didn't believe him, but I opened the doors anyway.

What I saw broke me.

When I finally opened the doors again, he had laid out hundred-dollar bills like flower petals. A trail of money across the floor, the couch, the table.

He called it love.

I knew it was a ransom.

Then came the casino. The ID check. I was underage.

And for the first time in forever… someone made me leave.

That woman at the slot machine didn't know it, but she saved my life.

I left with $20,000—and a heart that finally understood how expensive peace really was.

4. The Whisper That Saved My Life

The arrest wasn't a fall—it was a rescue in disguise.

I was in Tennessee on another job. But something was off. The atmosphere was too still. Too strange. Then came the whispers—soft, but sharp. Like divine warnings:

"Take the SD card out of your tablet."

"Wear flats."

"Leave a note for housekeeping. Let them know you'll be back.

I didn't know why. But I obeyed.

That night, I walked into a sting. Cuffed. Alone. Humiliated.

They let me go hours later. No money. No ID. No plan. Just me on a dark street with a torn-up soul.

And then out of nowhere—another whisper.

"Call a cab."

I hesitated. Again.

But I listened.

The cab driver looked me in the rearview mirror and said words that felt like thunder:

"Nothing in your life will go right until you go back home and do what God told you to do."

He dropped me at a hotel. Paid for several nights. Handed me cash. Said to call when I was ready to fly home.

Then he vanished.

To this day, I believe he was an angel.

5. The Room Where I Died and Lived Again

That hotel room? Sacred ground.

Four days. No noise. No distractions. Just me and God.

I cried. I prayed. I rocked myself to sleep. I begged for answers. I screamed into the sheets. I wrestled with demons that had lived inside me for decades.

And then I made the covenant:

"God… if You take care of him—cover his mind, body, and spirit—I'll go home. I'll leave everything. I'll do what You asked."

I didn't bargain. I surrendered.

When I got back to Philly, I told my folks that God said I had to leave. I expected a fight. I expected for me to have to make an enormous amount of money before he'd allow it.

Instead, he took a couple shots of Henny, and he paid for my flight in silence.

And then the phone rang.

It was my mother. We hadn't spoken in years.

She said:

"God told me to tell you—nothing in your life is going to go right until you go back home and do what He told you to do."

Same words. Same timing. Same God.

I wept.

Because that's when I knew… this wasn't a coincidence.

This was divine order.

6. Grief, Grace, and Getting Back Up

The return wasn't easy.

Healing felt like dying.

I missed the chaos some days. I missed the numbness. But God was doing heart surgery, and I had to let Him cut.

I sat in that room and laid down every version of myself that had been forged in trauma.

The hustler.

The fixer.

The broken little girl who always had to be strong.

And in her place, God raised up a new woman.

Not soft. Not weak. But holy.

Set apart. Sent back to the very women I once stood beside in silence—to tell the truth.

I didn't just survive.

I transformed.

7. The Hope Dealer Is Born

I started writing. Not for fame. Not for money. For survival.

Journals turned into revelations. My pain became purpose. My notebooks were stained with tears, scriptures, visions. Every page was a war. Every sentence, a sermon.

Women started listening.

Started crying.

Started saying, "You too?"

They didn't need a perfect leader. They needed a real one. And that's what I became.

Not because I planned it. But because obedience made me dangerous.

I spoke the parts most people leave out.

I exposed the wounds others covered up.

I stopped pretending.

And God gave me the mic.

Now I teach women how to heal out loud.

How to fight with faith.

How to walk out of hotel rooms and into holy ground.

8. From Hotel Floors to Heaven's Doors

I am not who I used to be.

I'm not the girl who cried in the backseat before going to make money.

I'm not the woman who mistook manipulation for love.

I am a mother raising seven kids. A vessel. A voice. A walking miracle.

I don't write because I want to inspire people.

I write because I don't want anyone else to bleed in silence.

This isn't a testimony. It's a movement.

This isn't a sob story. It's a survival manual.

This is the beginning of The Hope Dealer Collective—a sacred space for women who are ready to walk out of survival mode and into their supernatural identity.

And this is just the first page.

Final Words: The Wilderness Was the Way

If you are reading this and you're still in the middle of your own wilderness—

Don't quit.

Don't numb it. Don't glamorize it. Don't run from it.

God is doing heart surgery.

Let Him.

Let Him break what's killing you.

Let Him whisper what you won't say out loud.

Let Him become the only voice you obey.

Because on the other side of the breaking is abundance.

And I'm living proof that He still meets His daughters in hotel rooms with no phones, no plans, and no options—and crowns them in glory.

Stay close.

Because next?

We're walking through your wilderness together.

My upcoming The Hope Dealer's Guide to Healing Journal and Companion Workbook will guide you—page by page—through your own sacred healing.

This is the beginning of your comeback.

Let's go get your crown, sis.

Love,

Breauna Chante' ♡

The Hope Dealer

Founder, The Hope Dealer Collective

Chapter 8:

Built By The Battle

Nakisha Woods

A Warrior's Testimony Through the Battlefield

By Apostle/Coach Nakisha Woods

Opening Prayer

Heavenly Father, thank You for Your unwavering presence through every storm. Thank You for loving me so deeply that You gave Your only begotten Son, so I might have life and have it more abundantly. You have made me the head and not the tail, above and not beneath. I lift up the reader of this testimony—may a divine seed be planted within them, growing into strength, healing, and purpose in every season of their life.

Lord, through battles of addiction, abuse, and mental anguish, you have been our fortress. You have equipped us with Your armor, as declared in Ephesians 6:10–18:

"Finally, be strong in the Lord and in his mighty power. Put on the full armor of God, so that you can take your stand against the devil's schemes. For our struggle is not against flesh and blood, but against the rulers, against the authorities, against the powers of this dark world and against the spiritual forces of evil in the heavenly realms. Therefore, put on the full armor of God, so that when the day of evil comes, you may be able to stand your ground, and after you have done everything, to stand. Stand firm then, with the belt of truth buckled around your waist, with the breastplate of righteousness in place, and with your feet fitted with the readiness that comes from the gospel of peace. In addition to all this, take up the shield of faith, with which you can extinguish all the flaming arrows of the evil one. Take the helmet of salvation and the sword of the Spirit, which is the word of God. And pray in the Spirit on all occasions with all kinds of prayers and requests. With this in mind, be alert and always keep on praying for all the Lord's people." In Jesus name we pray amen. (biblestudytools.com)

A Heart of Forgiveness

Before I begin, I want to clarify: I harbor no hatred toward men or my ex-husband. Sometimes experiences shared in my chapter may be painful, but my intent is not to condemn. Rather, I aim to illuminate the realities of toxic relationships and domestic violence, emphasizing the necessity for intervention, love, and healing within our communities.

The Beginning of Love

In 2005, I fell deeply in love with a man I had known since my teenage years. He was hardworking, family-oriented, and respected. At the time, I was a single mother of one precious daughter, pursuing a degree in Criminal Justice at California State University, Sacramento. Our relationship blossomed quickly, and we moved in together, trusting the foundation of our long-standing friendship.

One evening, while waiting for him to return home, I read 1 Corinthians 13:4–8, reflecting on the nature of love:

"Love is patient, love is kind. It does not envy, it does not boast, it is not proud... It always protects, always trusts, always hopes, always perseveres. Love never fails."

I realized that my love had become all-consuming, leading me to compromise my values. He had become an idol in my life, which is a sin, as stated in Exodus 20:3–5:

"You shall have no other gods before me... You shall not bow down to them or worship them."

Anything-or anyone—that takes precedence over God becomes an idol.

The Struggle Within

Reflecting now, I see how I allowed my emotions to dictate my actions. In moments of conflict, I would hastily say, "Get out!" I was not building my house with wisdom. Proverbs 14:1 teaches:

"The wise woman builds her house, but with her own hands the foolish one tears hers down."

A wise woman nurtures and strengthens her home through godly wisdom, characterized by love, patience, and faith. In contrast, a foolish woman may unknowingly cause harm through negativity, disrespect, or neglect of spiritual priorities.

Our relationship was fraught with contention from the start. I was entangled, tolerating mistreatment and being disrespectful towards my ex, but I believed love would conquer all. This cycle persisted for 20 years, encompassing dysfunction, anguish, and abuse.

Yet, I serve a God who transforms battles into testimonies. He protected me through storms of domestic violence, infidelity, and public humiliation, allowing me to become a vessel to guide others toward healing.

Purpose in Pain

Romans 8:28 reminds us:

"And we know that in all things God works for the good of those who love him, who have been called according to his purpose."

This verse assures us that God is sovereign, orchestrating every circumstance for our ultimate good and His glory.

On our wedding day, before we could even consummate our vows, my husband was arrested for a probation violation. In front of our children, family, and friends, he was taken away from us, just moments after we said, "I do." Despite the shock, pain, and public embarrassment, I chose to stay. I had made a covenant before God to honor my husband in sickness and in health, until death do us part. For the first eight months of our marriage, he was incarcerated. During that time, I stood by him—writing letters, making visits, raising our children, and working two jobs. That season, though painful, forged **resilience** in me and prepared me for the battles still to come.

Embracing Resilience

Resilience is the capacity to recover from adversity. In my journey, it manifested through:

- **Emotional Strength**: Managing emotions while providing stability for my children.
- **Adaptability**: Adjusting to new family dynamics and responsibilities.
- **Support Systems**: Relying on community and faith-based resources.
- **Faith and Optimism**: Maintaining hope through a personal relationship with God.

Through prayer and divine guidance, I navigated these challenges, emerging stronger and more grounded in faith.

Recognizing the Cycle

After my husband's release, our marriage oscillated between moments of peace and turmoil. Unbeknownst to me, we were trapped in the cycle of domestic violence, that looked like:

1. **Tension Building**: Stress accumulates, leading to increased irritability.
2. **Abusive Incident**: Tension erupts into abuse—physical, emotional, or psychological.

3. **Reconciliation**: The abuser apologizes, creating hope for change.
4. **Calm**: A temporary period of peace before the cycle repeats.

Each cycle eroded my self-esteem, leading to trauma bonding—a psychological attachment to the abuser. Through therapy and spiritual growth, I recognized these patterns and began the journey toward healing.

Empowered by Faith

1 John 4:4 offers reassurance:

"You, dear children, are from God and have overcome them, because the one who is in you is greater than the one who is in the world."(bible.com)

This verse affirms that God's power within us surpasses any external force. Through Him, we can overcome adversity and find peace.

Breaking the Cycle: A Journey of Healing and Faith

I once believed that my experiences were isolated incidents, not realizing the deep-rooted historical and generational factors influencing the cycle of domestic violence in my life. Born into a family where conflict was normalized, I was exposed to domestic violence even before birth. My mother, pregnant with me at 14, endured abuse that, unbeknownst to me, would imprint itself on my being, lying dormant until it manifested when I was 27.

Each time the cycle repeated, I found myself asking: Why couldn't I love in a healthy way? While my ex-partner certainly played a role in the dysfunction, I had to confront my own. I made the choice to stay, to participate, to endure. As women, it's vital that we take accountability for our actions, not in shame, but in truth. When we embrace responsibility and extend grace to ourselves, we open the door to healing, even in the midst of chaos.

I often questioned how I found myself trapped in this harrowing cycle and whether escape was possible. Amidst the turmoil, I sought solace in God, finding refuge in my workplace, grateful for a safe haven. Reflecting now, I recognize God's unwavering protection over me, my children, and even my ex-partner during those tumultuous times.

I don't place blame solely on my ex; we both carried the weight of unresolved childhood traumas. Our relationship became the crucible for my healing journey, revealing wounds I believed were healed.

During my academic journey at California State University, Sacramento, I had the pleasure of taking an Ethnic Studies course titled "The Black Family in the United States," which illuminated the systemic dismantling of Black family structures. Let's delve into this further:

Historical Disruptions: Slavery and Its Aftermath

During slavery, African American families were often forcibly separated, with individuals sold without regard to familial bonds. Legal recognition of marriages among enslaved people was nonexistent, leading to fragmented family units. Post-emancipation, many sought to reunite with lost family members and establish legally recognized marriages. However, the legacy of these disruptions had lasting effects on family cohesion and structure.

Breaking the Cycle: Understanding the Roots of Domestic Violence in the Black Family

Historical Disruptions—Slavery and Its Aftermath

"My people are destroyed for lack of knowledge." – Hosea 4:6 (KJV)

Before we can truly heal, we must understand where the pain began. For many Black families, the legacy of slavery and systemic oppression has left invisible wounds that still bleed into our homes today. Historical trauma contributes to domestic violence, and how we, as women of faith, can confront these truths to break generational cycles and embrace restoration.

Broken Foundations: The Disruption of the Black Family

Reflection:

During slavery, Black families were intentionally separated. Men were stripped of their roles as protectors and providers, while women were exploited physically and emotionally.

Impact Today:

This created generational confusion about roles, trust, and connection within the family. When family bonds are not honored or protected, dysfunction takes root.

Scripture Reflection:

"If the foundations be destroyed, what can the righteous do?" – Psalm 11:3 (NKJV)

Understanding the Scripture

"Foundations" represent the core structures upon which life, families, and society are built — such as truth, justice, love, identity, and God-ordained order.

When David asked, "What can the righteous do?" he wasn't suggesting hopelessness — he was calling attention to the **urgency and crisis** that happens when what is *meant to be stable* has been **shaken or destroyed.**

Connection to Slavery: The Destruction of Foundations

Slavery violently uprooted the God-given foundations of the Black family and community.

◆ **Family Structure Destroyed**

- Husbands were separated from wives.
- Children were sold away from their mothers.
- Generations lost the model of healthy relationships and protective family bonds.

◆ **Identity and Dignity Erased**

- Names were stripped.
- Cultures were silenced.
- Self-worth was crushed by systemic dehumanization.

Slavery didn't just steal people—it stole the very *foundations* of what it meant to be a whole, loved, and safe human being.

Generational Impact on Domestic Violence

The ripple effect of broken foundations caused by slavery still affects Black families today:

- **Unhealed generational trauma** leads to cycles of anger, abandonment, and dysfunction.
- **Misunderstood roles in relationships** create confusion around love, respect, and power.
- **Poverty and systemic racism** add pressure and stress that often erupt in the home.
- **Silence and shame** keep victims from speaking out, and communities from healing.

When the foundation of a home is cracked, what's built on it eventually suffers.

What *Can* the Righteous Do? (The Answer in the Scripture)

The question in Psalm 11:3 is rhetorical, and the answer is found in the rest of the Psalm:

"The Lord is in His holy temple; the Lord's throne is in heaven: His eyes behold... the righteous Lord loveth righteousness." – Psalm 11:4–7

- **God is still on the throne** — He sees it all, and He cares about justice.
- **The righteous must rebuild** — We are called to be *repairers of the breach.*
- **Healing begins at the root** — By going back to what was broken, we can allow God to restore.

Healing Declaration

"I acknowledge the broken foundations of my family, my history, and my heart.

But I declare that through Christ, I will rebuild.

I am the cycle breaker. I am healed. I am restored.

My legacy will be built on truth, safety, and love."

Reflection Prompts:

- What "foundations" in your life or family do you feel were damaged or destroyed?
- How has the legacy of slavery affected your understanding of love, protection, or family roles?
- In what ways can the Church help rebuild what's been broken?
- What is one foundation you want to re-establish in your home

Violence as a Learned Behavior

Reflection:

Slavery normalized physical punishment and control. Enslaved people were disciplined through violence, and this behavior became part of the survival framework passed down through generations. The practice of **physical punishment and control**, especially within the Black family, often has roots that are both **historical** and **cultural**, shaped by trauma, oppression, and survival. Below is a breakdown of **where physical punishment and control deriving from**, with insight into its connection to slavery, generational trauma, and the need for healing

"What's passed down isn't always what's godly."

Slavery: The Origin of Physical Control

Historical Context:

During slavery in America, Black people were controlled, broken, and "disciplined" through brutal beatings, public punishments, and violent authority structures. Physical punishment was used as a **tool of control** to dehumanize and force obedience.

- Enslaved parents were powerless to protect their children from this brutality.
- Some began to **adopt the master's methods** to discipline their children as a means of survival, believing that "if I beat you, you'll learn before the white man beats you worse."
- This gave rise to the mindset: **"I discipline you out of love to protect you from the world."**

But love that imitates oppression can never lead to true freedom.

Generational Trauma and Survival Parenting

Trauma teaches urgency, not tenderness.

Physical control and harsh discipline became **generational tools** passed down from grandparents to parents to children, not always out of cruelty, but out of fear, pain, and a desire to protect. Many Black parents disciplined with severity because they believed:

- "The world won't give you grace, so I won't either."
- "If you don't listen to me, the police or the streets will handle you worse."
- "I have to break your will before the world breaks you."

This parenting style often comes from **unprocessed trauma**, not biblical love.

Cultural Misinterpretation of Scripture

"Spare the rod, spoil the child" is NOT in the Bible—but it's been misquoted and misused for generations.

The Bible **does** speak of correction (e.g., Proverbs 13:24), but it never promotes violence, shame, or fear-based control. Misapplying scripture has justified physical punishment, even when it causes emotional or physical harm.

True discipline in Scripture means **teaching, guiding, and correcting in love**, not abuse or domination.

Power, Pain, and Patriarchy

In many communities, control is equated with strength. Those who feel powerless in society (due to racism, economic struggle, or lack of opportunity) may seek to regain a sense of authority **at home** through control, dominance, or intimidation.

- Men raised in environments where masculinity is defined by aggression may use force to assert control.
- Women, especially single mothers under stress, may discipline harshly to maintain order.

But control rooted in pain breeds more pain.

The Call to Break the Cycle

Jesus didn't rule through fear—He ruled through love.

The way forward is not to beat pain into our children, but to **build safety around them.** We must name these roots of trauma, unlearn harmful patterns, and return to God's model of discipline:

- Patient correction
- Loving boundaries
- Grace-based growth
- Emotional safety

Scripture for Healing:

- *"Fathers, do not provoke your children to anger, but bring them up in the discipline and instruction of the Lord." – Ephesians 6:4*
- *"There is no fear in love. But perfect love drives out fear." – 1 John 4:18*
- *"The Lord is compassionate and gracious, slow to anger, abounding in love." – Psalm 103:8*

Healing Reflection

"I release the belief that control is love.

I will not carry the trauma of my ancestors into my children's future.

I choose healing, grace, and Spirit-led guidance in my home."

Impact Today:

Some have unknowingly repeated these behaviors, using violence to express control, dominance, or unresolved anger in relationships.

Affirmation:

I break the cycle of generational violence. I walk in love, power, and a sound mind. – *(2 Timothy 1:7)*

3. Unhealed Generational Trauma

Reflection:

The trauma of slavery never truly ended, it simply evolved. Economic oppression, racism, incarceration, and lack of access to mental health care created a culture of silent suffering.

Impact Today:

This unresolved trauma may lead to unhealthy emotional coping mechanisms, including domestic violence, substance abuse, and relational dysfunction.

Prayer Prompt:

"Lord, heal the wounds I didn't cause but have carried. Break every curse that seeks to pass through me."

The Pressure of Provision and Protection

Reflection:

Society emasculated Black men, then labeled them "angry," "absent," or "abusive." In response, some overcompensated with control or aggression.

Impact Today:

Distorted views of masculinity contribute to toxic behaviors, and many women carry the weight of protection alone. I would like to dive a little deeper into that point.

"Distorted views of masculinity..."

This refers to **unhealthy, culturally or generationally taught ideas** about what it means to be a man.

Examples include:

- "Real men don't cry."
- "Power = dominance."
- "Manhood is proven through control, aggression, or sexual conquest."
- "To be weak is to be less than a man."

These distorted ideas often stem from:

- **Historical trauma** (slavery, racism, fatherlessness)
- **Media influence** (glorifying hypermasculinity)
- **Peer pressure or upbringing** (boys being punished for showing emotion)

. "...contribute to toxic behaviors,"

When masculinity is misunderstood or misused, it can lead to behaviors like:

- **Domestic violence** or emotional abuse
- **Neglect of family responsibilities**
- **Inability to communicate feelings in healthy ways**
- **Dominating or controlling women and children**
- **Fear of vulnerability, leading to isolation or substance abuse**

Toxic behavior is not about being a man — it's about **misusing one's identity in ways that hurt others and self.**

. "...and many women carry the weight of protection alone."

Because of these toxic behaviors and broken family structures, **women are often left to:**

- Protect themselves **physically and emotionally**
- Raise children on their own, **guarding them from harm**
- Serve as both **provider and nurturer**
- Defend themselves from **harmful partners or systems**
- Create boundaries while longing for support

This creates **emotional exhaustion** and even **resentment**, and leads to deep trauma when women feel they must be strong all the time with no rest or refuge

When manhood is misdefined as dominance or emotional detachment, it fosters harmful behaviors. As a result, women are often forced to step into roles of protector and provider alone, carrying burdens they were never meant to carry without partnership and covering.

Reflection:

What false roles or expectations have you carried that God is calling you to release?

The Silence that Hurts Us

Reflection:

Historically, Black women were told to be "strong," to "keep the family together," and to "protect our men." While noble in intention, this has caused many to suffer in silence.

The stigma around reporting abuse continues to silence victims, often trapping them in unsafe situations out of fear of judgment, rejection, or disbelief. I can relate deeply to this. I didn't want my ex-partner to go to jail or be punished—I wanted him to be healed. When the police were finally called, I felt overwhelming guilt. As agencies like CPS, the Sacramento County District Attorney's Office, the Family Justice Center, and the grassroots organization EMPACT became involved, that guilt only intensified. I felt like I was violating "hood politics," but at the time, I believed this was the only path to safety.

Even with that choice, I endured further trauma. Some agencies viewed my case through a rigid, black-and-white lens, forcing me to advocate for myself constantly. I lived in fear that missing a single appointment or deadline could lead to harsher consequences. Amidst all this, EMPACT stood out as the only organization where I felt completely safe and supported during my healing journey.

Scripture Reflection:

"There is a time to be silent and a time to speak." – Ecclesiastes 3:7

I thank God for giving me the courage to speak up and share my whole truth and testimony finally. My story is authentic, not rooted in bitterness, but in healing. I've seen both sides of domestic violence, and I choose to speak from a place of grace, not resentment.

Healing Path Forward:

- **Acknowledge** the historical pain but refuse to be imprisoned by it.
- **Accept** accountability, not blame—our healing starts with honesty.
- **Align** your identity with Christ, not your past.
- **Act** in love, truth, and grace—one step at a time.

Closing Declaration:

"I am the cycle breaker. I am the healed. I am the restored. I am the woman God is raising up for such a time as this."

Pressure at Home: Economic Challenges, Migration & the Rise of Domestic Violence

When Survival Becomes a Silent Struggle

Theme Scripture:

"Come to me, all who are weary and burdened, and I will give you rest." – Matthew 11:28

Financial Stress as a Trigger for Conflict

When families are living paycheck to paycheck, stress levels skyrocket. Financial insecurity can lead to feelings of failure, inadequacy, and hopelessness, particularly for individuals who are expected to be providers.

When someone feels powerless financially, they may try to assert control in other areas, often through emotional, verbal, or physical abuse. Financial arguments are one of the leading causes of domestic conflict.

Reflection:

How do you handle financial pressure in your home? Do you feel safe discussing money with your partner?

Unemployment and Role Reversals

When men are unemployed or underemployed while their partners are working, it can trigger an identity crisis, especially in a society that expects men to be the "breadwinner." This imbalance can lead to feelings of emasculation, frustration, and eventually, resentment. When my husband went to jail in 2008, it began a long season of unemployment for him. He stayed home to care for our growing family while I worked, holding down two jobs and building my career. Yet, my ex had been working since the age of 16. In fact, I was the one who took him to his very first job interview. Imagine his frustration. Even though he gave me his blessing to pursue work and advancement, I believe over time, resentment began to take root.

Power struggles and insecurity may arise, and in extreme cases, they may manifest as controlling behavior, jealousy, or abuse. Women may also experience burnout and emotional exhaustion, feeling unsupported and stuck.

Scripture Reflection:

"Better is a little with the fear of the Lord than great treasure with trouble." – Proverbs 15:16

Housing Instability and Overcrowding

Migration and poverty often force multiple families or generations into tight living quarters. A lack of privacy and personal space can lead to frustration and frequent conflict.

Tension builds easily in overcrowded homes. Children witness more arguments. Emotional and physical boundaries are more complex to maintain. This environment becomes fertile ground for toxic behaviors.

Prayer Prompt:

"Lord, make room for peace in our homes, even when space is tight. Let Your presence dwell where chaos once lived."

Migration and Displacement

When families move—whether to escape violence, seek better opportunities, or flee instability—they often lose access to support systems like extended family, church, or community services.

Isolation increases vulnerability. Without strong social support, victims of domestic violence may feel trapped, unable to ask for help or unaware of local resources.

Affirmation:

I am not alone. God goes before me and surrounds me. I am supported and seen. *(Deuteronomy 31:8)*

Systemic Barriers and Discrimination

Discriminatory hiring practices, wage gaps, and generational poverty disproportionately affect Black families. These systems are often invisible but deeply felt—limiting upward mobility and intensifying household stress.

Frustration with society often bleeds into the home. When external systems deny power, some individuals attempt to regain it within the family—sometimes by force or manipulation.

Scripture Reflection:

"We are hard pressed on every side, but not crushed...struck down, but not destroyed." – 2 Corinthians 4:8–9

Healing Path Forward:

- **Educate** yourself and your loved ones on the warning signs of economic-based domestic violence.
- **Empower** women and men with financial literacy, job training, and access to safe community resources.
- **Equip** your home with emotional tools—grace, communication, and accountability.
- **Encourage** seeking help—not as weakness, but as wisdom.

Declaration for the Home:

"We will not be ruled by fear or lack. Our home is a sanctuary, our family a team. God is our provider, and peace is our portion."

Invisible Chains: Systemic Racism, Discrimination & Domestic Violence

When the System Fails, the Family Feels It

"Speak up for those who cannot speak for themselves; ensure justice for those being crushed." – Proverbs 31:8 (NLT)

Domestic violence in the Black community doesn't happen in a vacuum. It is often the fruit of deeply rooted injustice systems that were not designed to protect or uplift Black families. Generational wounds caused by racism and discriminatory policies continue to fuel cycles of trauma, control, and silence. In this session, we name those systemic roots and reclaim our power through truth, faith, and healing.

Mass Incarceration and Fatherlessness

Black men are disproportionately arrested and incarcerated due to over-policing, racial profiling, and harsher sentencing. Many households are left without fathers, husbands, or sons, leaving emotional and financial gaps.

The absence of a stable male presence can lead to economic hardship, stress, and loss of protective relationships in the home. Boys without healthy male role models may repeat cycles of anger, abandonment, or control. My ex's parents divorced before he was a teenager. He did not witness a healthy male role model growing up.

Scripture Reflection:

"God sets the lonely in families, he leads out the prisoners with singing." – Psalm 68:6

Lack of Access to Mental Health & Legal Support

Reflection

Racism has created fear and mistrust of law enforcement and social services. Many Black women avoid calling the police during domestic violence situations, fearing for their partner's life or their own.

Fear traps victims in abusive homes. Lack of culturally competent mental health services makes it harder to process trauma or access healing.

Prayer Prompt:

"Lord, make our homes safe again. Let justice flow in our communities. Let healing rise from the ashes in Jesus' name, we pray, amen

These systemic factors began in slavery in most cases of domestic violence in black families. Exploring each factor gives us history and insight as the WHY? Why must be addressed as we endeavor to rebuild the structure of African American families. Here's what I found on the tragic reality of

Data regarding **Black women killed by intimate partners in Sacramento County** over the last five years:

Key Statistics (2019–2023)

Disproportionate Homicides Among Black Women (2024 Data)

- In 2024, Sacramento County recorded **20 female homicide victims**, at least **6 were Black women**, all shot to death (theguardian.com).
- Black residents comprised about **11%** of the county population, yet represented **~50% of total homicide victims** (theguardian.com).

Historical Context: Intimate Partner Homicide Trends

- Since **1987**, more than **300 people** in Sacramento County have been killed by intimate partners—an average of **~10 per year** (pmc.ncbi.nlm.nih.gov, centerforhealthjournalism.org).
- Women are nearly **four times more likely** than men to be killed by a current or former partner (centerforhealthjournalism.org).
- Black women were **overrepresented** among these victims, more than **25%** of partner-homicide victims, despite being only ~10% of the population (theguardian.com).
- **National Numbers Show the Same Trend**
- Nationally, from **2018 to 2021**, Black women accounted for **~30% of intimate partner homicide victims**, while representing about **8% of the U.S. population** (en.wikipedia.org).
- **Gun Violence & Domestic Homicide Link**
- In the broader state context, women in relationships where the partner owns guns are **five times more**

likely to be killed, and from 2013–2022, **83% of domestic violence gun homicides** were female victims (sacobserver.com).
  - Black victims accounted for **13%** of these fatalities statewide, while comprising just **5.7%** of California's population (sacobserver.com).

Summary of What This Means Locally

Why This Matters for Healing and Advocacy?

- **Invisible emergency**: While community gun violence gets attention, domestic violence homicides—especially against Black women—often go unnoticed in prevention strategies (theguardian.com).
- **Healing requirements**: These statistics underscore the critical need for culturally responsive, faith-based healing programs, legal protection, and community support.
- **Collective responsibility**: Tracking and publicly discussing these numbers brings light and accountability—it's a first step to restoring theguardian.com.

I was a single mother when I met my ex, reliant on assistance programs, with my name alone on our lease to benefit from reduced rent. My past experiences of being expelled from home as a teenager ingrained in me a mindset of self-reliance. Instead of communicating my emotions healthily, I suppressed them until they erupted in anger. As previously mentioned, I would often ask my ex to leave, sometimes for safety reasons, but this pattern ultimately eroded our family unit. I believed I held power, but it was an illusion fostered by a system that equipped me to function independently of a man. Rather than uniting us, it drove us apart. Healthy love is attainable, but now I understand the divine order: God – Husband – Wife. I was meant to find shelter in my husband, not hide from him.

I chose to deepen my relationship with Christ, allowing Him to rebuild me in the midst of my battles. I was broken down completely so God could mold me into the warrior I am today. Every tear shed was purposeful. I turned inward, releasing blame and resentment toward my ex-husband. As I grew closer to God, I began to see him through Christ's eyes. (thetimes.co.uk)

Eventually, we joined a church in Sacramento, California. My ex embraced salvation, and our lives began to transform. The pastor, aware of his past, welcomed us warmly, and we renewed our wedding vows in a beautiful ceremony. We attended Bible study and marriage counseling together. During this period, I was trained in the power of prayer and spiritual warfare, becoming wholly devoted to Christ. God was working within me.

I immersed myself in prayer books on spiritual warfare, realizing I was engaged in a battle for our family. I began waking at two or three in the morning to pray over our home, my ex, and our children. However, as my ex's church attendance waned, the abuse resurfaced. Between 2010 and 2023, we separated ten times, each instance triggered by domestic violence. Initially, church attendance brought respite, but the closer I drew to God, the more our relationship deteriorated.

Colossians 2:6-7 states:

"So then, just as you have received Christ Jesus as Lord, continue to walk in him, being rooted and built up in him and established in the faith, just as you were taught, and overflowing with gratitude."

Our spiritual journey requires deep roots in Christ, building upon our faith, and expressing gratitude.

I endured immense physical and mental turmoil, reduced to a state where I could only rely on God. Once, while showering at his mother's house, he dragged me out, berated me, and demanded I leave with our two young children in the middle of the night. With minimal gas and WIC vouchers, I drove to WinCo Foods, terrified and in tears. Though I had family, I hesitated to involve them in our chaos. I cried out to God for direction, and He led me to a high school friend's home, where I stayed for weeks. Unbeknownst to me, we were entering the honeymoon phase again. He resumed church attendance, promised therapy and counseling, and I believed him. I returned, and the cycle persisted for years.

As I continued to pray, praise, and worship, the Holy Spirit transformed me. I assumed leadership roles in our church, was promoted to Human Services Coordinator at work, and was blessed with two more daughters after a miscarriage caused by being thrown down stairs. Despite the pain, God opened doors no man could close.

I delved into scriptures on forgiveness, determined not to become a bitter woman. The more I studied, the more God surrounded me with uplifting individuals. I managed a successful program for the City of Sacramento, earning several awards. Despite my home life, I maintained professionalism at work. My mother and uncle began attending church and gave their lives to the Lord. Friends sought me out for prayer and godly counsel. I was appointed Children and Youth Director at my church, and sometimes, the children's service had more attendance than the main congregation. It was nothing but God. I refused to dwell in pain and pity. My extended family began asking me to pray before dinners and gatherings. I started waking up for intercessory prayer times, leading prayer calls, and fully surrendering everything to God.

At a cousin's engagement party, after praying, I escorted my grandparents to their car. My grandfather, a man of great stature, looked down at me and said, "Little Bit, you have the GIFT." "Little Bit" was his nickname for me. I had no idea what he meant. I turned to God, seeking understanding of the gift my grandfather mentioned. During this time, I attended workshops to equip me for intercessory prayer, and it was then that I heard the voice of the Lord welcoming me into his kingdom as a Minister.

Conclusion: Built by the Battle

That was only the beginning.

You see, I didn't grow up in church. I had only ever been a member of one—Antelope Upper Room Ministry under Pastor Juanita Mason, Sacramento, CA. When I first began to hear the voice of the Lord, I had only been there three years. Doubt clung to me like a shadow. I thought: *I didn't go to theological school. My past is messy. My marriage was falling apart.* Why would God choose *me* to teach and preach His Word?

One phrase I often heard in my spirit was, "God doesn't call the qualified—He qualifies the called." Though not a direct scripture, it echoes the truth woven throughout the book of Exodus. Moses—the man who led an entire nation out of slavery—doubted himself, too. In Exodus 4:10 (NKJV), he says, *"O my Lord, I am not eloquent… but I am slow of speech and slow of tongue."* I didn't stutter like Moses, but I wrestled with a deep sense of unworthiness. I had battled anger, depression, and low self-esteem, and I was a late high school graduate. I didn't feel equipped or eloquent, but the call was undeniable.

God had been with me since my mother's womb. Jesus protected me through every violent incident with my ex. In the chaos, He was my peace. In the darkness, He was my light. When I read Exodus 3:11-12, where Moses asks, *"Who am I that I should go to Pharaoh?"* and God replies, *"Certainly I will be with you,"* my spirit leaped. That verse carried me through the earliest days of ministry, reminding me that *God was always with me.*

When the final incident with my ex occurred in late 2023, I realized every battle had prepared me for *this* purpose: to help others break free from domestic violence. Just five days later, I received a heartbreaking text from a sister-friend who had just survived a horrific attack by her husband. Immediately, I stepped in to advocate for her. It wasn't my flesh that responded—it was the Holy Spirit. Years of prayer, study, and submission to God's Word activated in that moment. I was being *built by the battle.*

Most people don't understand the depth of healing that freedom from domestic violence requires. It's not a "one and done" solution. It takes therapy, intercession, advocacy, and consistent love. The spirit of domestic violence is demonic, and it's taken too many of our families. We must call it out and engage in spiritual warfare. *Our weapons?* The power of prayer. Decrees. Declarations like Isaiah 54:17— *"No weapon formed against you shall prosper…"* I clung to that promise. And Romans 8:28 reminded me that *all things work together for the good of those who love God and are called according to His purpose.*

Even in the turmoil, God allowed me to build. I launched **Keys2Victory Coaching and Empowerment Institute**. I became a five-time author. I coached over 50 women leaders to rise in their callings. The battle didn't break me—it built me. God preserved my mind, my purpose, and my peace.

In early 2024, I received a message that rocked my soul: *"Sister, it is time. It's time for you to be affirmed as the Apostle you are."* I had been walking in that office for years, but in 2024, I was officially affirmed. An apostle is a "sent one"—a representative. And I know now, without a doubt, that I was sent by God.

As I close this chapter, my heart overflows with gratitude. God, thank You. Thank you for keeping me. Thank you for never leaving or forsaking me. Thank you for renewing my mind, protecting my children, and doing exceedingly, abundantly above all I could ask or imagine. In Jesus' name, Amen.

To whoever is reading this: *Whatever battle you are facing, seek the Lord and allow Him to shelter you through it.* I can now say with confidence that *I am free.* The residue took time, but with wisdom, therapy, and God's grace, I found wholeness. I forgave my ex—, I refused to carry bitterness. The enemy planned to leave me broken, addicted, and angry—but *God* had another plan.

Many are alive in body but dead in spirit because of the silent torment of abuse. My healing wasn't linear. It took a village: therapists, pastors, sisters, and the community. But God's plan prevailed.

I also recognize that many systems and agencies are not equipped for the level of trauma survivors face. One local Sacramento agency, alongside two others, became my support. Through that experience, I became a **faith-based domestic violence advocate** and birthed Keys2Victory Ministries.

Yes, I was broken. Yes, I was bruised. But I was *built by the battle.*

And I live to testify—*God still heals. God still delivers. God still sends.*

Glory to God

Restoration and Forgiveness

I would be remiss if I didn't share that the weight of domestic violence deeply impacted our entire family. In the summer of 2024, one of our middle daughters began struggling under the influence of what I can only describe as demonic spirits—confusion, rebellion, rejection. I believe the absence of her father's consistent presence and her longing to be seen and heard opened the door for these influences. It eventually came to a head and exploded in our home. In a moment of desperation and discernment, my ex, her father, was called—and that phone call became the starting point for our family's restoration.

We share something sacred—our children. And nothing, not even the pain of the past, can change the fact that we are their parents. One day, our children will have children, and I want my grandbabies to know what healing looks like. I want them to experience a family that may not be traditional, but is whole, united, and anchored in peace.

By the grace of God, we now share space peacefully and respectfully in the presence of our children. That may seem small to some, but to me, it's a miracle. I never imagined my nervous system could feel calm enough to be in the same room with my ex. But our children are witnessing something powerful: a mother and a father who chose forgiveness. We may not have gotten it right as husband and wife, but we're choosing to get it right as parents, as people, as believers.

The culture promotes division, but the Kingdom promotes restoration. The world will tell you to cancel and cut off, but God says to forgive, extend mercy, and love anyway. The battle didn't just shape my ministry—it gave birth to it. I now serve as an **Apostle of Love, Keys2Victory Ministries, Sacramento, CA,** not because I've mastered perfection, but because I've surrendered to healing. The battle made me approachable. It softened me. It gave me compassion for the broken, the abused, the angry, and the ashamed. I can now invite others into a relationship with the ultimate Healer—Jesus Christ.

The battle also allowed me to re-evaluate my love for myself. I used to *love myself* in theory, but now I'm *in love with Nakisha.* There is a difference. I honor her. I protect her peace. I speak life over her daily. The scripture that now rests on my heart is the same one I began with at the start of this chapter; however, now, with a deeper personal relationship with Christ, I apply 1 Corinthians 13:4-8 to my love walk with myself.

"Love is patient, love is kind..."

Real love isn't rushed or reckless. It doesn't intimidate, pressure, or harm. Love takes its time to listen, to care, to nurture. Love is *kind*, not cruel. If you are constantly being insulted, manipulated, or physically harmed, that is not love—it's control, fear, or trauma.

"...it does not envy, it does not boast, it is not proud."

Love is secure, not jealous or possessive. If your partner tries to isolate you, accuse you unfairly, or control who you talk to, that's not love—it's insecurity masking itself as ownership. Love is humble—it doesn't puff itself up or make you feel small.

"It does not dishonor others..."

Love doesn't humiliate you, belittle you, or make you feel worthless. Any relationship that brings constant shame or disrespect is not founded on godly love.

"...it is not self-seeking..."

Love doesn't make everything about one person's needs or desires. In abusive relationships, the abuser often centers themselves and expects the world to revolve around them. That is not biblical love. Love gives, it doesn't take advantage.

"...it is not easily angered, it keeps no record of wrongs."

If someone is exploding in anger, threatening you, or bringing up your past mistakes to manipulate you, that is not love. Real love is slow to anger and doesn't keep score.

"Love does not delight in evil but rejoices with the truth."

Love does not celebrate abuse, secrecy, or manipulation. It doesn't cover up wrongdoings or excuse bad behavior. Love *rejoices with the truth*, and sometimes that truth is this: "This is not safe. This is not love."

"It always protects, always trusts, always hopes, always perseveres."

God's love is a *protector*. If you're being harmed—physically, emotionally, spiritually—that is not protection. That is harm disguised as love. God's love shields, supports, and creates a safe space for growth and healing.

"Love never fails."

God's love never runs out. It doesn't flip on you. It doesn't hurt you. It doesn't fail you.

If what you're experiencing doesn't line up with the *fruit of love* described in this scripture, I want you to know—you are not crazy, and you are not alone. Abuse is never God's will for your life. You were created in His image, fearfully and wonderfully made. His love is gentle, faithful, and healing. You deserve love that reflects His heart.

If you're struggling with leaving or unsure of what steps to take, that doesn't make you weak. It makes you human. But know this—**you were not built to live in fear, shame, or violence**.

There is hope. There is help. And there is a future beyond this pain.

And above all, **you are deeply loved.**

Heavenly Father,

I come before You on behalf of Your daughter, the one who is tired, broken, and questioning her worth. Lord, wrap her in Your perfect peace. Let her know she is not forgotten, not forsaken, and never unloved. You see her pain. You've counted every tear, and you are near to her even in this dark season.

I pray You break every chain of fear and confusion. Silence the voice of the enemy that tells her this is all she deserves. Remove the shame, the guilt, and the lie that she is not strong enough to leave or heal. You, O God, are her refuge, her defender, her shelter in the storm.

Speak to her heart. Help her hear Your voice above all others. Remind her that she is fearfully and wonderfully made, chosen, and deeply loved. Reveal to her a safe path forward. Raise up a village of people who will walk with her in truth, healing, and love.

Father, I declare freedom, protection, and restoration over her life. May she walk boldly into her next chapter—whole, healed, and held by You.

In Jesus' name, I pray, amen.

Love didn't fail me.

God didn't fail me.

And I pray you will come to know that He won't fail you either.

The battle built me, but grace restored me.

And love? Love is what now leads me.

Made in the USA
Las Vegas, NV
20 November 2025

34759867R00095